BULLARD'S BEST

Bullard's Battle
Book #9

Dale Mayer

BULLARD'S BEST (BULLARD'S BATTLE, BOOK 9)
Dale Mayer
Valley Publishing

Copyright © 2021

ISBN-13: 978-1-773364-93-3
Print Edition

Books in This Series:

About This Book

Welcome to a new stand-alone but interconnected series from Dale Mayer. This is Bullard's story—and that of his team's. All raw, rough, incredibly capable men who have one goal: to find out who was behind the attack on their leader, before the attacker, or attackers, return to finish the job.

Stay tuned for more nonstop action as the men narrow down their suspects … and find a way to let love back into their own empty lives.

After finding the killer who'd tried to take out the entire team, and now with Bullard safe, the crew heads back to the island where he recovered. Leia wants to get married there, so Dave has gone ahead with Katie, Bullard's caterer, to set things up.

Dave has a new lease on life, now that Bullard is safely back home, and fixes his sights on an old friend he's always kept slightly distant. Katie has been in Dave's orbit for a long time; she's not sure what's changed in their relationship, but something certainly has, and she couldn't be happier.

Except for one loose thread from that same island. After all, someone let the outside world know Bullard was alive. Someone they had yet to find. So a week in paradise might start with some time in hell first.

CHAPTER 1

DAVE MONTGOMERY ARRIVED separately at the island two days ahead of the rest of the team. He walked through the tiny village, stopping specifically to see the medicine woman to pay his respects.

The old lady looked up at him, her face a plethora of wrinkles, layered on top of each other in every direction. But that gaze of hers was deep, dark, and direct. She smiled. "She's okay now, isn't she?"

"She is, indeed. They'll be back here in a couple days." He added, "Not to stay but for a visit."

"Visits are good." The old woman nodded. "She can't stay here anymore."

He looked at her in surprise.

She shook her head. "It's another stage of her life. She needs to move on."

"I think she's ready to move on now too," Dave agreed, but that didn't mean he thought anybody else would. "I wanted to thank you for all the help that you gave her over the years."

The old woman looked at him and cackled. "She's been good for us. She's a healer. There are never enough."

He nodded, looked around. "Somebody here betrayed her and told the outside world and the men hunting her."

The old woman nodded. "Somebody, but I don't know

who."

He didn't know whether he should believe her or not. At the same time, Dave wanted to make sure no ugliness surfaced during the visit for the upcoming wedding ceremony. "I want to make sure she's safe when she comes back here."

"I have no issues with her. She's been good to us here." The medicine woman stopped and thought for a moment, then frowned. "Did Terk find her with her kidnapper?"

"Terk sent us in the right direction to locate her."

The medicine woman craned her neck, her gaze studying his face. He felt almost like a probe was searching his brain to make sure he had told the truth. Then she nodded. "Good. Terk is very strong, but he will need help."

"In what way?" Dave asked cautiously. Terk was one of those guys who never asked for any help, and you never quite knew when he needed anything—other than to have people heed his warnings. But he always seemed to know when any of the team needed help.

She looked up at him, still prodding Dave with her gaze.

He frowned, hating the uneasiness that coursed down his back. "Terk knows he can call us if he needs something."

She nodded. "You look after her now."

"We will," he replied. "They're coming here to get married."

At that, her face blew up into a beautiful smile. The layers of wrinkles were rearranged somehow, and the weariness of her face now became radiant.

"I wanted to invite all of you to her wedding. She became very close to you over the years that she was here."

The medicine woman nodded and smiled. "We will be there." Then she started to laugh. "It will be a big wedding."

"I don't know about that." Yet his mind prepared to add to what some of the guys had planned.

"Oh, it will be." She continued to smile. "You just don't know it yet."

"I do know of some ideas and plans in play, but I don't know that anything will come of it."

She just smiled and waved him off.

"We also need to know, when she leaves her island home, that it will be safe and ready for her, when she wants to return."

"We are not thieves," she stated. "We appreciate all she's done for our people here, and she is more than welcome to return, whenever she so desires."

"Thank you." As he turned, he looked around, not yet leaving. "I have a friend coming in to help with the cooking and the setup."

"She's not just a friend, I see."

Dave heard her but continued past that remark, not sure the old woman was speaking of Katie. "We'll park a yacht just off Leia's place."

She nodded. "Good. You will be bringing lots of people then."

"We will try not to interfere with your way of life."

She laughed. "You already have." Then she smiled again. "It's good. For the town and for Leia. Now you must focus on Katie."

Dave frowned. He had never mentioned her name to the medicine woman.

But she smiled and repeated, "Yes, Katie is good for you."

With that, Dave turned and headed over to Leia's place, thinking about the old woman and her remarks about Katie.

Leia's place was about a forty-minute walk from the main part of the village, where the old medicine woman lived. Leia was far enough away to be alone, and far enough away that, when something went wrong, she was in trouble. Still, she'd survived a lot of years here on her own.

But Katie would arrive before Leia did. Dave picked up the pace to be sure to be there for her, when she reached land.

As he walked toward the waterfront, where Bullard had spent those months recovering, Dave remembered what Leia had said about building a bed and a shelter around Bullard because he was too big to move. As Dave stood here and stared, he realized how true it was, and now that he knew, he could envision it. He just whistled because, without Leia telling him, Dave had already figured that Leia had gone to ingenious lengths in order to save Bullard. He was a huge man. Dave himself wasn't small, by any measure, but to move someone, when they were injured and a dead weight like that, was almost impossible. How Leia, as small as she was, had moved Bullard, even as much as she did, was an amazing feat.

Dave and Bullard went back years, decades. Bullard had been with Dave when he lost his leg. Nothing Bullard could have done about that, given that a blast had been involved in severing his limb, but Bullard did save Dave's life. And, when Dave lost his wife and daughter, Bullard had been there for Dave too. For the initial shock of that dual loss and for each of the many days thereafter. Dave now wondered if Bullard had put his life on pause because of Ice ... and because of Dave. He sure hoped not. Having a wingman all these years, as both men remained resolutely single and unattached, yet loving people out of their reach, had been a balm to Dave.

But he hoped Bullard hadn't done it just for Dave.

He shook his head, bringing this new clarity to his personal history, where he sheltered himself from future agonies. Did he really hold any devastation at bay by doing that? Or did he just reject any happiness along with the hurts? If so, it was time for him to embrace a new future, like Bullard.

That man was a force of nature. Dave had shared many ops with Bullard, and seeing him in action was death-defying. However, an unconscious Bullard, who couldn't help anyone, not even himself? That thought scared the hell out of Dave. Thankfully Bullard had landed in Leia's lap. Dave shuddered to think of the alternative ending, where Bullard had been found by anyone else.

Dave walked from the beach, where Bullard regained his strength, to the shelter, where he had lived for four months, while convalescing. Leia never explained how she had managed to drag Bullard this far. Probably some adrenaline surge, like reading about a mother lifting a car off a child.

Not knowing much about Leia but having spent years admiring Katie's ingenuity, Dave knew what Katie would have done, faced with moving an unconscious Bullard. She would have constructed a sled out of all the available brush around here, with a rope attached to her waist and the sled. Dave laughed out loud, all by himself, just at the thought of Katie pulling that off. Much like Leia must have.

Katie was a loner too. She worried Dave at times, like when she went to feed the homeless on the streets, handing out leftover food after each event she catered. He kept telling her to check in with him before she did this and again when she returned home again. She would say, "You worried about me, Dave?" in that teasing voice of hers. Hell yes he was. But she never called him. "They know me, Dave. I'm accepted there." Much like Leia was accepted here in the village.

Except for the one guy who had sold her out.

As Dave turned, he saw a yacht anchored a good one hundred yards offshore. He lifted an eyebrow to stare at it closer. Then he saw a small boat puttering toward the shore. He walked down to the edge of the beach and waited for it. And then he smiled.

It was Katie. Alone. She was fearless. She raised a hand in greeting.

He helped her out of the boat, saying, "You'll get wet."

"In a place like this? I would hope so. This is absolutely stunning." She walked up on the shore and stared at the view. "This is really where he was for all those months?"

Dave nodded. "Insane, isn't it?"

"It's more than insane." She chuckled. "Talk about being lucky."

"Of all the things that Bullard is," Dave agreed, "lucky is definitely one of them."

She smiled and nodded. "What do we have for facilities?"

"It's worse than I originally thought," he admitted, "and I'm sorry about that."

She looked at him with that unwavering smile. "Show me."

On the way to Leia's cook cabin, Dave gave Katie a tour, pointing out where Bullard had done his healing, while they had been searching for him, fearing the worst. Dave explained how Leia had built the bed and shelter up around him, and together Dave and Katie imagined how difficult it must have been.

She shook her head in awe. "That is one determined

woman."

"I know." Dave smirked. "She's very much in love with the man now, but, back then, he was just a near-dead stranger she found in the ocean."

"Hard not to love Bullard," Katie replied lightly. "He's a good guy."

"Oh God, does that mean you're in love with him too?" Dave's tone was joking, but inside he wondered because he'd heard that same sentiment from so many different women over the years.

"Nope, not like that," she corrected, with a shake of her head. "He's an all-around good guy, definitely a good boss man too, though not somebody you'd want to cross. Yet underneath all that, he is definitely all heart."

"I know." Dave smiled and then walked up to show her the cabin, where Leia had stayed all these years.

Katie stepped inside, turned around to take it in. For a Spartan cabin, Leia had made it a very feminine and yet utilitarian space somehow, with drapes of mosquito netting and brightly colored cushions. When they got to the small corner where Leia had cooked, Katie frowned and winced. "Wow, if she fed herself by cooking on this for all those years, she deserves a medal for that too. But to feed Bullard as well? That is amazing." She shook her head.

"I don't imagine it was easy, but she did have access to supplies from the mainland," he reminded her. "Plus, a lot of fresh local fish is around here, and the village has its many gardens, and she was probably trading her medical services to help them out in return for foodstuffs for her use."

"Right, but still a lot is lacking here," Katie noted.

"Only for a big celebration," he pointed out. "For daily living, especially such a simple life, it was probably easy enough to manage."

"I'm jealous, actually," Katie admitted. "I can't imagine how joyful it would be to stay here, to live so simply, even for a week or two."

"We're working on purchasing other properties here." He stood tall, hands on hips, taking in this part of the island. "So, if you ever want to come and stay for a while, I'm sure that can be arranged."

She looked at him in surprise. "Why are you guys buying land here?"

"Leia doesn't want to let go of this special place, where she got the respite and the peace that she needed to heal," he replied quietly. "This is also where she and Bullard met and spent all that time together. And, day by day, she brought him back to life."

"She's a romantic," Katie noted.

"Bullard too. The first thing he did when they got safely home was buy up the adjoining land, so we all could come here for holidays. Now he's just waiting on the paperwork to make it legal."

She chuckled. "Yep, he's a romantic too."

"What? Does that mean you're not?"

"Of course I am." Katie shrugged. "I'm female. That almost goes with the territory, for most of us anyway."

He laughed. "So, will you make this work?"

"Do I have any choice?" she asked.

"Not really," he said, with a laugh.

"In that case, I can make it work." She spun around the tiny cabin, frowning. "But, if we're talking food for three meals a day for a lot of people, over several days, we'll need a decent amount of supplies."

"We can get supplies brought up to the yacht on a daily

basis, so I don't think that's an issue."

"Not when you've got money," she noted. "In that case, you can do pretty much whatever you want."

"Oh, good." Dave gave a nervous laugh. "I was worried I might have set you up for a big pain in the neck."

"No, it'll be fine, but all the trouble that happened here, all the danger here has passed, right?"

"Yes, for the most part. Leia and Bullard both had enemies after them, and both have been dealt with. Now somebody here on the island betrayed her, whether a local or from the mainland, which is how the word got out that the two of them were here, but we're not exactly sure who that was and what it was all about. Money probably."

"Hopefully you get it resolved before too long," she said, her gaze steady on Dave. "The last thing I want is to have anybody disrupt our time here."

"Do you think you'll have time to actually enjoy yourself?"

She turned and looked at him in surprise, then laughed. "Honestly, I should be thanking you guys and doing this for free. The idea of spending time here right now is fabulous, but I do still have to work for a living." Katie turned that cheeky grin of hers on Dave. "So, thank you for using my services and not somebody else's catering company. I'll kill you if you try to change it now."

"No change needed." Dave smiled, his hands up in mock surrender. "Bullard is always really happy with your food."

"I do cater for him quite a lot." She turned to look at him. "So, how are you holding up anyway?"

"Me? I'm doing well. Why do you ask?"

"I just wanted to make sure that you're doing okay with

cus."

at her in surprise.

gged. "I don't know all the particulars, but it
. the two of you have both been single for a long
time. . not always easy to watch somebody who's kind of
been your wingman, so to speak, suddenly find somebody
special."

"Bullard really needed this," Dave acknowledged. "He's
been so focused on his work, living only half a life for a long
time, always hankering after something he couldn't have.
Knowing the score but incapable of changing it. That
situation was hard on everybody, seeing Bullard not truly
happy and settled in life." As soon as the words were out of
his mouth, Dave knew they applied equally to him. Another
revelation as to his own life.

"And sometimes we only hanker after what we can't
have because we can't have it," she reminded him. "It's a safe
way to do nothing."

He smiled. "Either way, Bullard is over the moon in
love, and I am delighted for him." He said it in a firm voice,
and he hoped she believed him because he was very happy
for Bullard. Did it highlight Dave's own situation? Absolutely. As he studied the woman in front of him, he realized that,
although they had become good friends, they hadn't really
gotten any further than that.

Was Dave interested in pursuing his relationship with
Katie further? Yes. Was this spurred on by Bullard's love for
Leia? Probably. Was Dave finally taking a critical 360-degree
look at his own personal life? Definitely. If Bullard could
find a love that rivaled his idyllic love for Ice, then what were
the odds that Dave could find a love that equaled or eclipsed
his love for his wife and daughter? Maybe better than he

thought. Dave finally saw hope, saw possibility, saw how he had limited his life.

Now, more than ever, Dave really wanted a chance at forever with Katie.

KATIE HAD BEEN crushing on Dave since the first time Bullard had hired her and had introduced her to Dave to assist in that initial catering job—and many others since. That was so many years ago. She shook her head at that. Why hadn't she spoken up way back when? She could have asked him out, after all. She didn't know what held her back exactly.

At that meeting eons ago, before Bullard even spoke, Katie caught her first-ever glimpse of Dave, feeding a stray dog what looked like homemade dog biscuits. This huge battle-scarred warrior had a soft spot for animals. It still brought tears to Katie's eyes when she remembered that fateful day. And he continued to show her his sensitive side, not being all about ego and alpha-male superiority, even though Dave was just as confident and as fully male as Bullard.

Katie had learned much more about Dave over the years. He was all about saving the planet, not disrupting Mother Nature, treating Earth with the respect needed to further our human race. He got especially irate when dealing with continuing crimes against women and children—raping, trafficking, abusing.

As Katie had listened to him telling tales over the years, without giving too much away, she had learned that he was a medic—or more. Katie wasn't sure exactly the depths of his training, on any level, but, in the medical realm, he seemed to have learned a lot from Bullard. They both knew how to set up a bare-bones clinic in the most desolate of regions. And had done dozens, if not hundreds, of them, training the locals to take over in their absence or when short a traveling doctor.

Those two were a humanitarian force unlike any other she had seen up close and personal.

Dave was different from Katie in so many ways, yet, in others, they were more alike. He could cook too. So they shared that skill. And he was a kind soul, despite the harsh events in his life. The test of life had proven over and over how Dave was a good man, how Dave never faltered from his core values, how Dave could be depended on without fail.

So, knowing all this, why did she hesitate to make her feelings known? Obviously the man was never spontaneous. He was cautious. Hell, the man was stagnant. And she was getting impatient.

She looked at Dave and wondered at what point in time he'd be ready to move on. She knew his history and wondered if he was just clinging to it because it was easy. That was a harsh thing for her to say, but she was so desperate for him to take a step in a new direction. She was really hoping, now that Bullard had found peace for himself and someone to love, that maybe Dave would be open to the possibility too.

But Katie wouldn't push it. Again she asked, *Why?* Was it some old-fashioned idea that the man had to ask out the woman, not the other way around? She had asked out other men before, but then ... look how those relationships had ended. Yet she didn't know them as well as she knew Dave. Was she fearful of being compared to his deceased wife? Sure she was. And living up to a ghost who just got more perfect with every day would be a losing fight for sure.

Playing devil's advocate with herself, she didn't think Dave was like that. Katie had seen him with his niece. Hell, she had seen him with Bullard and the team. How Dave reacted to servers at her catering functions with the same respect that he doled out to his fellow warriors. Dave had nothing but love in his heart. Sure, he had loss in his mind, but Katie felt like his heart would win out. She had been giving him time to work it out on his own schedule.

Bad move, she told herself, with a smirk. She had had no idea it would take him this long.

But, on the other hand, if Dave didn't know anything about how she felt, how could he deal with it? Sometimes men were dense. Plus sometimes it was just that male-female miscommunication thing happening. Maybe she just needed to be blunt. Put it out there. Let him decide, once he knew how much she liked him. If he agreed to further their relationship, it would be worth that moment of angst. Hell, she had been torturing herself about this for years. And if he didn't want more from her? Well, yes. That would hurt. But she could course correct, given some time to mourn the loss of a good man. A perfect man, in her opinion.

Time to man up, Katie.

She smiled at him and looked around at this beautiful, peaceful environment. Taking a deep breath, she decided there was no time like the present. Before she had a chance to talk herself out of it, she began. "I can see how Bullard's circumstances led him to rethinking his life, both on a personal level and a professional level."

"How does one really know, I wonder?" Dave asked curiously.

"I think you just find an opportunity where you want to explore moving forward."

"I've shut the doors for such a long time though. How do I even know when I'm supposed to open them?"

She looked up at him, smiled, gave him a gentle hug. "You'll know. Besides, it doesn't have to be an all-or-nothing deal. Taking a step forward doesn't mean you can't still look back."

He hugged her back almost fiercely, and she wasn't sure how much of that reflected his needs versus his fears. But regardless, she let him hug her.

When he was done, he stepped back. "I'm sorry. I shouldn't have done that."

"Absolutely you should have. Come on, Dave. If nothing else, we're friends, and we always will be."

He nodded and smiled. "We've been friends for a long time, haven't we?"

"We have." Maybe she had fears too to deal with—of ruining such a wonderful friendship by asking him out.

He grabbed her hand, and they walked back to the water. "It's very idyllic here, isn't it?"

"Can we trust it to remain that way over the wedding?" she asked seriously.

He looked at her, one eyebrow raised.

She shrugged. "I know a little bit about what you do, how busy your life is, and the type of work you are involved in. And I also know some of what happened here." She motioned behind her.

"We'd like to have a talk with one person, a local, but I don't know that it's anything to be worried about."

"Of course not, but maybe you should check it out anyway."

"Good point." He smiled. "So, do you need anything from me?"

"Yeah, your help with setting up and just transporting foods and tables from the yacht to the island."

"As always, you have that. What about right now?"

"Well, I need to sort out what I have on the yacht to bring here. We'll need an awful lot of tables, but we can do the bulk of the cooking there on the yacht and bring it up here."

"That's what I was hoping for, given the lack of a real kitchen on the island."

"Okay, I'll head out right now."

"Are there things here that we need?" Dave asked. "Like sourcing fresh fruit and vegetables from the village?"

She looked back up at the hill that led to the closest village, not quite an hour away, thinking of carrying all that produce back via carts and lots of walking, and then shrugged. "Not really. I think we'll use our own suppliers."

"Okay. Maybe I'll head to the yacht with you then."

"Sure, come on." She asked, "Are you planning on staying here?"

"I'm here for the wedding and a couple days afterward."

"In that case, you should stay on the yacht with me." She paused. "If you want to, of course."

He frowned and then shrugged. "I'm not sure what to say to that."

"What's the matter? Scared of being too close to me?"

He chuckled. "I'm sure you'll be gentle."

"What if I don't want to be gentle with you?" She raised her eyebrows.

He burst out laughing. "Did I ever tell you how much I appreciate your friendship?"

She nodded. "Yes." She wasn't sure what to say after that. Dave seemed not ready to date or just not ready to date her.

As they got back to the yacht, she returned to the friendly but strictly business relationship they'd had before.

By the time they had checked their inventory and evaluated what they might still need to pick up and bring out, they went over the menu.

"Now I understood I was here for four days, but, if you guys are staying here longer than that, do you want me to leave enough groceries behind?"

He tapped the tabletop and wondered. "I know that Bullard is planning on staying here a good ten days. And he was planning on flying in with a bunch of stuff."

"Of course." She looked around. "You guys need a dock for shipload deliveries. And a heliport too," she added on a laugh.

"We do." Dave nodded, all seriousness. "I think the guys will get together and build each while they are here."

"Of course they will," she said, with an eye roll.

He laughed. "Remember? With money and some serious skills, you can do anything."

"I know." She smiled. "Let me know what you decide on the food provisions thing."

"Will do."

CHAPTER 2

HOURS LATER DAVE got back onto the small boat with Katie, as she took him back to shore. Together, they walked up to the area slated for the wedding and the reception to take one more look and to check off a few things that she still had on her list. One of which was looking for some level space, trying to decide if there was enough room, or if they needed to build some deck space. They measured Bullard's shelter, as it could even be repurposed.

She walked inside, shook her head. "I still can't believe he stayed here all that time."

"It was a terrible situation that brought him here of course, but, in the end, I think his downtime here was something he was really blessed to have. He needed it for his physical health but also for his mental healing, aside from his brain trauma. I understand Leia was like a balm, both provoking and allowing Bullard some time for deep introspection. We are all so thankful that Bullard had Leia during his time here and now will have her evermore."

Katie sighed with longing, as she nodded and stepped out of Bullard's makeshift cabin. She walked over to where the river met the ocean water. "It's such a damn special space."

"It really is, and look at all this." He swung an arm

around this beautiful vista. "Hopefully this is a place that will stay this way." He nodded his head, deep in thought. "We want to keep this pristine for as long as we can. Bullard is buying this as much to preserve it as to set it aside for Leia and his team to use. Bullard will not trample on Mother Earth as he adds in some cabins for his people."

"Absolutely." Katie was glad to hear that, but she knew Bullard wouldn't destroy the land here as he didn't in Africa at his two compounds there. Over in the bushes something caught her attention, and she thought she saw somebody staring at them. She frowned. "Are there any neighbors?"

"No, not for miles."

"So we're being watched then," she murmured.

He looked at her and nodded.

"Okay then. I wondered if it was just me." She tilted her head. "We need to deal with that, preferably before all the testosterone arrives."

"Oh, we'll deal with it all right." Dave chuckled. "And I'm telling the team that you said that, by the way." Reaching out, he tucked her arm into his elbow. "Let's walk over in his direction."

"Is that wise?" she asked.

"Well, it's the best option we have at the moment," he murmured.

She frowned, and then together the two of them walked along the rocky edge that appeared to be more like steps.

"She had a beautiful five years here," Katie murmured. "I'm almost jealous."

"I know, right?"

DAVE WALKED CAREFULLY; his gaze ever watchful. He had

noticed the leaves rustling on the far side of the river earlier, but he hadn't known whether it was animal or human. There were several crude crossings, as in downed trees that allowed someone to cross. One had a rope as a guide farther up. He had already been here, exploring, but he hadn't seen anybody on this side. And because Leia didn't own the property on the other side—that was one of the parcels Bullard was trying to buy—Dave didn't really have any right to be there. Not yet.

Plus, Dave figured the island way would take longer to get the paperwork done, making this all legal. But given that most of the island on this side was deserted, Dave was less concerned about that issue and more concerned about everybody's safety. With Katie at his side, he walked forward, his gaze checking out the bushes.

"Do you think somebody is here?" she asked softly.

"I imagine so." He gave a subtle nod. "A lot of people live in the nearest village, and there has probably been a lot of curiosity about what's going on with Leia, especially since she left. Any activity here is bound to make a stir. People are naturally curious."

"Did they steal her stuff?"

"I had a crew come back here and gather up her personal belongings right after they left. As you can see, there's no way to lock up or to look after anything. But then the island people are not as concerned about possessions as other societies." He shrugged. "I think it's more about curiosity than anything criminal, like stealing."

"I get that, but we need to ensure the safety of everyone coming here for the wedding."

Dave agreed. He walked up to the first bridge. "Are you okay to cross this?"

"Sure. The worst that can happen is I'll get wet. Wetter, that is."

He just laughed, loving her openness. Still holding hands, the two walked across the makeshift bridge until they stood on the other side.

"I can't believe how beautiful this island is. Just compare this lush landscape to a new subdivision back home, where they plow down every tree and bush in sight, leaving desolation behind. And for what? To build a house amid a plot of gray dirt? It pains my heart to see the mindless death of all those trees. Why can't they take down a few trees to make room for the footprint of the house? Maybe use the downed trees for firewood for the new home or even for flooring in the new construction?" She shook her head, lost in those thoughts.

"Right. That's exactly why we are looking at this as being a vacation retreat for the company, getting back to nature, getting back to simple, getting back to wholesome, after dealing with the blights in the world."

"Works for me." She released another long sigh. "I would love to spend some time here. It's actually very romantic."

He chuckled at that. "There we are, back to talking about romance."

"Not sure there's any getting away from it." She laughed. "We *are* here for a wedding, after all. Plus, it's definitely gorgeous here."

And it was also empty of humans. "I'm not seeing any evidence of someone being here now," Dave noted.

"No, but, if they didn't want to be seen, it wouldn't be that hard to hide in this landscape."

"That's quite true," he agreed. "But, as far as I know, all

the bad guys have been caught at the moment."

"Excuse me if this is offensive, but, in your line of work, there appears to be a never-ending supply of bad guys."

"That is quite true." He gave her points for that. What he really didn't want was anything to interrupt the wedding or to cast a cloud over the visit for anyone.

"So are the rumors true? Are you really planning on having that many people get married that same day?" She paused, then added, "Not that it really makes a difference in my catering plans, other than having one wedding cake shared by all." She frowned. "Or I could do individual cakes …"

"Let me ask you about that." He stopped, turned to face her. "As a woman, do you think the women will feel put upon, if the guys spring this idea of getting married on them so quickly? Would it bother you?"

She thought about it, then shook her head. "No, but then I'm a person who likes to do things spontaneously, at least if I'm left in charge." She firmed her lips and gave a one-arm shrug. "So, for me, it would make a lot of sense to do something like this. While obviously I do make plans for my catering jobs ahead of time, I'm not the type to plan something for myself and have it be months away."

"Right, so you would prefer to have something that would come off fairly quickly."

"Absolutely. I'm not at all good at waiting," she admitted. "But I'm pretty sure I'm not your average female either."

"There's nothing average about you," he stated sincerely.

She squeezed his fingers. "Thanks. I think."

He smiled. "It was definitely intended as a compliment."

She wondered just how long they would tiptoe all around it. Finally she decided that, even though it could be awkward if the answers weren't what she wanted to hear; it would be worth it to get it resolved. Squaring her shoulders, she just said what was on her mind.

"So, Dave, are we heading somewhere, such as a dating relationship, or will we just continue to walk around it indefinitely?" She studied his face, seeing shock, then pleasure, washing over his features. She relaxed a bit, still nervous what he would now say.

"Well, I'd like to see us head somewhere," he replied, surprised by her directness. "I just don't want to push you or to make you uncomfortable."

"We've known each other for years," she noted. "Could a simple bit of conversation like this be pushing it?"

"Maybe right now it is." He explained further. "While we've got a lot of wedding-related work to get through over the next few days, plus we need to find the snitch and find out who is watching us, but going on a date or something down the road is certainly a potential."

She smiled and shook her head. "How about we forget about *dates down the road*. We've had plenty of time to get to know each other. So how about you have dinner on the yacht with me tonight? Let's just be crazy and call it a date. We're alone for the next two days, after all."

He looked at her, and a slow smile formed and spread across his face. "If you're asking me out," he teased, "I accept."

"Well, I guess that's one way to get a date with you." She laughed, happy he said yes without too much hesitation. "So will you come and stay on the yacht with me?"

"I wasn't really planning on it." He frowned.

"I think you should. That way we can have some wine and just relax. We can really get to know each other a little more."

"I'd like that a lot," he replied warmly.

She gave him a gentle smile. "Me too." And, with that, they took one last look at their lush surroundings and explored a little more.

Calling it a date made him feel awkward. Just calling it *dinner* made him relax a bit. Was he stuck in a rut? Probably. And an older man stuck in his ways was hard to prod along. He almost laughed out loud at that thought. Dave had never been a flirt. He was much too serious for that. But he was as honest and as honorable as the day was long. Maybe too honorable when it came to his late wife. So he was at a disadvantage here. He wasn't nearly as "in touch" with his feelings as Katie was.

Granted, as a male, he was told to tamp down his feelings, unless they were rage and anger. Not so much about tears and empathy. The military had furthered that mind-set too. Yet he knew, for all he had been through, the training and the tough personal years, he had retained his humanity. He was proud of that.

Still, he wasn't sure quite what to say or how to react to Katie and her honesty, but everything that they'd gone over so far matched what he already knew. She was a very independent and capable woman, and he liked an awful lot about her and enjoyed her company very much.

The fact that she was stunning and his type was something else in her favor. He noted a little flare of residual guilt about his wife, but, after all these years, the deaths of his wife and daughter had become a memory in the background that he refused to pull out anymore. He preferred to remember their lives and how special it had all been for the time they had shared. Was he ready to move forward? With Katie, most definitely.

Smiling, he added, "Well, I'd say, *I'll bring the wine*, but, in this case, I think you probably have something better."

"I definitely do. I can't believe you were even planning on staying here on the island, even in Leia's cabin."

He shrugged. "I've got my backpack. That's all I really need, and, hey, if it was good enough for Bullard ..."

"Well, you're a better man than I am," she stated. "There's not much in the way of running water and plumbing here, and the yacht offers that and much more."

"It does, indeed, and I'll gratefully accept your offer."

"In that case"—she smiled broadly—"why don't we head back there now?"

"Sounds good." And he led the way back to Leia's place, crossing over the same natural bridge again.

Katie glanced behind her. "Don't look now, but we're being watched."

"I felt it too. The trick is whether we'll have company who faces us or if it's just somebody being curious."

"It doesn't feel curious to me." She shook her head. "There is an ugliness to it."

Dave moved forward, careful of what he thought of as his bum leg, which really meant the prosthetic, wondering if she actually knew about it, yet thinking that she must, after all the many years they had spent working together. "Go ahead in front of me," he said, "just in case."

She looked at him in surprise, and he just shook his head and tucked her up in front, so that his body blocked hers. Once on the other side, she moved quickly toward Leia's hut and the accompanying beach. "We can't let anything mess up this special day for Bullard and Leia and however many others who are participating." She turned to ask him, "When are the guys coming?"

"In two days," he replied.

"Could they come sooner?" she asked nervously. "At least a couple of them? It seems like maybe we should get some things squared away before the whole group gets here. Certainly before Leia arrives."

"Yeah, I'll take care of doing just that. Pulling out his phone, Dave quickly sent off some text messages.

Fallon replied first, with a phone call. "Hey, Dave. Sounds like we need to check out things there and make sure nothing's going on."

"Well, definitely something *is* going on. I just don't know if it's ugly or not."

"Can you do a full search today?"

"Yeah. I'll send Katie back to the yacht. We were just assessing what we needed to do for the wedding, and we've had company watching us. I didn't see them, but I'm sure of it."

"Right," Fallon noted. "I'll see what I can do about moving up the timetable, for at least some of us anyway. I'll get back to you when I figure it out. Stay safe until then."

Glad to have reinforcements on the way, Dave slipped his phone in his pocket. "Come on, Katie. Let's get you back to the yacht, and then I'll return to the island to do a full reconnaissance."

She frowned at him.

"It'll be fine." He gave her a reassuring smile. "This is what we do."

Just then a shot rang out. They both reacted quickly, dashing a short distance, and diving to the ground at the water's edge. He managed to get her up into the transport boat, then down on the floorboards. Crouching outside of the boat, he pushed off and jumped inside. Firing up the motor, they were out of handgun range within seconds.

CHAPTER 3

KATIE STARED AT Dave, as they both remained low in the boat, waiting as it quickly pulled away from the shore. "Oh my God," she breathed. "They fired at us, didn't they?"

"Yeah, but that was no warning shot." His face was grim, as he pulled out his phone and sent Fallon a message.

As they continued to putt along, she asked, "Shouldn't we be at the yacht by now?"

"We're not going there," he explained. "I want to check out the coastline."

She stared at him in shock. "But, in the yacht, we can get away."

"We're out of danger and getting away just fine right now," he stated. "What I don't want to do is lead them to the yacht, so they know for sure that that's where we are. Obviously they'll know we could be there, but, if they don't see us heading that way, they may not attack it."

"Attack?" she repeated faintly.

"Yeah." He shook his head. "But I can't guarantee either way."

"I don't like talking about attacks." Her phone rang just then, with a text message. She pulled it out. "It's the captain on the yacht, asking what we're doing."

"Tell him what happened. He knows the drill."

She quickly sent a message, as best as she could, asking if he saw a shooter. He did not and included a warning to stay safe, saying he'd have the engines running, just in case. "He's warming up the engines, getting ready for a getaway—or to come pick us up, if requested."

"Good enough." Dave peered over the edge of the boat as he directed it around to the far side of the island. "I don't see anybody along here."

She frowned. "The village is on the other side though, right?"

"It is. This is the deeper area by the cliffs. On the other side they have a beach, so it's easier to bring boats in and out."

"Right. So, Leia's got a little bit of beach there, but mostly it's deeper water. I hadn't considered that."

"The rocks just drop way down," he noted. "Better for big boats, worse for smaller boats."

She smiled at that. "So, better for us if we wanted to bring the yacht closer."

"I was just wondering about that. Part of what I could do is check to see if we could anchor the yacht somewhere close by. Obviously it wouldn't be close enough to run a gangplank or anything," he said, "but, if we'll be building a dock anyway, it could help."

"Well, you won't go out very far with a dock."

"Yes, but, if it's really deep here, we could do a floating dock at the end," he suggested. "It's just part and parcel of the logistics we have to take into account because, if we'll be coming here on a regular basis, it will need the same security and accessibility as every other place we go."

"It's hard for me to imagine, but you guys all function as such a big machine."

"We do, indeed. And that's a good thing."

"If you say so. Do you think it's safe to sit up now?"

"Oh, I wouldn't," he said cheerfully. "We don't know what other kind of firepower they may have."

She groaned. "So, once you've checked out this section, then what?"

"I'm coming up around the side where I expect to see the island open up more to the beach area." He shifted, and she watched as he rose up ever-so-slightly and adjusted his position. He sat on the bottom of the boat, reaching up to steer, but he could see over the rail.

Following his example, she shifted too. "It's so beautiful. How can there be such danger here?"

"I think it must still be connected to Leia somehow."

"So, do you think that whoever it was who exposed her location to her kidnapper is the one causing the trouble?"

"I'm sure he thinks that us being here is a problem," he stated. "Imagine if you'd done something like that. Wouldn't you be looking over your shoulder to see if the people you sold the information to were coming back to clean up their loose ends or if the person you betrayed was coming back, seeking revenge?"

"Or, as in this case, we're coming back because we love the area but now are fully aware that somebody sold information about us."

"Which means, in many ways, that we should suspect everybody," Dave murmured. "When you're talking about an environment like this, secluded as it is, in an area where money is hard to come by, you have to expect that people could be talked into doing an awful lot for some cash."

"It still sucks," she muttered.

"More than you will hopefully ever realize." But then he

smiled. "Don't worry. It'll all be good."

"I don't know," she said, shaking her head. "You'll have to fix all this in the next two days, before I'll be doing any wedding catering."

"We will," he replied cheerfully. "Not to worry."

She groaned. "Says you."

"Is Sam the captain on the yacht?"

"Yes, it's Sam. How—"

"Text him to contact Bullard and to let him know what's up."

"Okay." Soon her phone kept buzzing back and forth, as she messaged Sam. Then Dave's phone buzzed. "Oh, so they've switched to talking to you now."

"Yeah." He groaned. "It's definitely part of the deal, but a little inconvenient to text while steering a boat from the floorboards."

"If it keeps me out of the middle of it, I'm happy. I don't really need to be involved in this part."

He looked at her. "Why not? You make a killer quiche."

She stared at him and started to laugh. "Oh my God. If that was supposed to be funny, that's really sick humor."

"Hey, anything to lighten the atmosphere."

"We could have been killed," she whispered.

"We could have, yes," he stated matter-of-factly. "Believe me. That's pissing me off more than you can imagine."

"Yeah, I guess you didn't travel all this way in order to get shot to death."

"It's not about me. It's you. I feel terrible and never intended for a moment to put you in danger. I just didn't expect any real threat remained here."

Her heart warmed at the thought. "It's very nice that you worry about me," she said. "And I have to admit that I wasn't expecting any danger. I've been looking at this as a paid vacation. Plenty of work to do, of course, but a fabulous setting. I just assumed, when the threats against Bullard and Leia got resolved, all the trouble was over with, and it would all be good."

"After we got Leia back from the kidnappers, we had a team come here and collect her personal belongings, her ID, clothes, things they thought she may need or want," he told Katie. "But I don't really know what the end result of that was. I didn't ask if they had any harsh words with any locals or if anybody tried to stop them while they were here."

"Surely they wouldn't be so foolish as to do that, would they?"

"You'd hope not," he replied, "but people will be people."

"Isn't that the truth."

DAVE REALLY HADN'T expected any danger here and was pissed at himself that he hadn't done a more thorough security check of the island when he had first arrived. But then again, he had done a cursory check and hadn't found anybody on Leia's land or any signs that he could see of vandalism. But he'd then gone to the village and been seen there, so the word would have gotten out that he was around. Was his presence causing a problem for someone? He frowned at that, wondering whether the old woman was behind it or if she was in danger herself.

Something like that would make Leia very unhappy. She had grown quite close to certain people on the island. She'd helped deliver several babies, had set a few broken bones, and had looked after several children with fevers. In all cases receiving food as payment, and she did regular doctor visits for other food supplies. At the same time, Dave had to consider that some people resented her. He hated for that to be the case, but not everybody held outsiders in high esteem. But none of this gave him any reassurance that something wasn't going on locally. That gunshot had been all too real. He pulled up along one of the village piers and tied up.

Reaching out a hand, he said, "Come on. We'll go talk to the medicine woman."

She looked at him in surprise. "Why?"

"To see if she knows what's going on."

"What if she's the one behind it?" Katie asked bluntly. "Maybe she was jealous of Leia's healing skills."

"That's possible. In which case, we need to go check it out."

"That's a little disturbing though," Katie said.

"It's all disturbing."

"You don't really think of guns in paradise."

"Sorry, but we'll have to now."

As they walked forward, several people stopped and stared. He had a smile on his face, and he made sure he was holding her hand.

"Your grip is a little tight," she noted. "Are you thinking that I'll run away or that somebody will try and snatch me?"

"Leia was kidnapped from here, so it's a little hard for me not to worry."

She squeezed his fingers gently, continuing, "I'm fine, and I do know some self-defense. You know that Bullard requires it of anyone working with you all."

"I know," he muttered. "But that gun wouldn't have given a shit who had self-defense training or not. The bullet was intended to take us out permanently."

CHAPTER 4

N O POINT IN arguing with Dave because, of course, he was right. Katie did tighten her grip on his fingers as they walked through the village. She had a smile on her face, but she didn't know how to react when no one smiled back. Were these people not used to seeing strangers, not used to seeing tourists, or just naturally suspicious?

"I wonder if this is how they initially treated Leia," she murmured.

"She was here long enough to get past their defenses and to actually became a friend to many of them," he quietly answered. "We are strangers at the moment."

"I guess," she said. "It would be easier if Leia were here, wouldn't it?"

"Without a doubt," he murmured. "Not to worry. We're not here to hurt them."

"Do they know that though?" she asked. "It doesn't really feel like it."

"Maybe not, but, at the same time," he added, "they'll see us over and over again, so they'll have to get used to it."

They walked up to the old woman's space, she had a small hut on lower stilts than many others. Katie looked at it. "I just can't imagine what it'd be like to live here year-round."

The old woman cackled from behind a post, and then

she leaned over and stared at them. She looked at Dave and smiled. "You're back again."

"I am"—he grimaced—"and the reason is not as nice as before."

She stared at him, with that all-knowing gaze, hitting Katie oddly. The medicine woman then studied Katie and back to Dave. "You two are as meant to be."

He shook his head at her. "I don't know what that means."

She smiled and looked at Katie. "You do."

She flushed. "I'm not sure that I do."

The old woman smiled again. "You do, but you're not there yet."

Not sure what she was talking about but afraid to ask for more details, Katie just ignored that possible romantic subject. "Somebody tried to kill us."

The old woman's eyes widened and went almost sightless; they turned nearly black. Then she slowly nodded. "And still the influences affect us."

"We were wondering if anybody here ..." Dave's voice trailed off helplessly because he didn't want to insult her by asking if anybody here would have shot at them. That is exactly what his words would do, but he needed to know, nonetheless.

"Maybe."

Her answer was a surprise. He stared at her. "Maybe?" he asked cautiously.

Katie squeezed his fingers. "Maybe what she meant"— she crouched in front of the woman—"is that money isn't evil here. They see much in the outside world, when they go to the mainland, and they want more."

"Yes." Dave paused. "And it doesn't take much to twist a

young mind into wanting more."

"Exactly," the old woman said. "But it's not necessary for all."

"No, of course not," he agreed. "And we don't want to insult you by assuming or accusing anyone."

"No," she murmured, shaking her head. She sighed. "I will ask questions."

"Of?"

She just waved a hand, and it was almost as if they were being sent away.

Katie looked at Dave, then back at the old woman. "I don't know what you want us to do," Katie said quietly. "We're scared to stay because of this shooter. I was nearly killed."

The woman looked at her with a frown; then she looked at the ground.

"More people are coming, you know? Including Leia," Katie added. "This needs to stop."

"Yes. Go now." The old woman turned to stare sightlessly in a direction that didn't include either of them.

Dave straightened and tugged Katie gently to her feet.

She looked at him and frowned. "Is the conversation over just like that, and we're supposed to leave?"

"Looks like it. She may already know who to talk to."

"It's a little odd though," Katie noted.

"It's more than odd, but this is the way of the island. Leia was comfortable here, and they were good to her."

"Until they weren't. Somebody anyway," she reminded him. "But we don't know for sure that it was somebody from the island. Someone may have come over from the mainland, realized something was going on, and decided to capitalize on it."

"True."

With a last glance, they turned and walked back through the village toward their boat.

As they got closer, he noted several men gathered around their skiff. "I hope they're leaving the boat alone."

Katie looked out to the water to see the men surrounding their boat.

Dave walked closer and called out, "It's our boat."

One of the men just looked at him and frowned.

Dave looked back at him. "What?"

But the man shrugged and backed off. Dave untied the boat and motioned for Katie to get in. When he looked up again, he saw the men staring at him. "Are you always this unfriendly to Leia's friends?"

Hearing the doc's name, they frowned again, and then one started to speak with animation.

When Dave didn't understand what they were saying, one of the other men translated. "They're asking if she's coming again."

He nodded. "Yes. She'll be here in a few days."

At that, their faces broke into broad smiles, and they stepped away from the boat.

"So does her name open doors for this place?" Katie muttered to Dave.

"Possibly," he replied. "I don't know what's going on."

"Not sure we're supposed to either." But she gave a bright smile and spoke to the crowd. "Leia is looking forward to coming home."

The men nodded. "We miss her."

"Yes. She's a wonderful lady."

And, with that, they carefully turned on the engine and pulled away from the dock, heading back around to Leia's corner.

"That was a very strange affair," Katie noted.

"Clearly they don't like outsiders," Dave stated.

"You can't really blame them. And Leia?"

"I don't think she counts as an outsider to them."

"But is that how they treated her too, at least at first?"

"Not now, but they may have originally. You can hardly blame them. People come here who like to exploit them. If not them personally, then I'm sure many a land developer had his sights on defacing the beauty of these islands into some concrete jungle. You can reverse the damage, but I'm sure it takes years or decades. Still, the loss of all that natural beauty is painful to bear, even in theory, much less before our very eyes. So I'm sure it took a long time for them to become comfortable with her presence."

"I guess we are safe now, assuming they steer clear of the yacht."

"I'll assume so," he said. "But whoever the gunman was, he isn't necessarily associated with the island. We have to remember that. Boats come back and forth all the time, and these people all have family, likely many of them on the other side of the mainland."

"Good point," she muttered. "So, in other words, nothing is for sure."

"Often it isn't."

THEIR DATE NIGHT had been set aside, with Sam and Dave and even Katie taking shifts aboard the yacht as lookouts during the night, as Sam steered the yacht into deeper waters. The next day, Sam dropped off Dave and Katie once again on the island, where they were stayed busy taking measurements and getting things set up and ordered. And Dave was thoroughly enjoying working with Katie.

Something had changed in their relationship. It went a little deeper that night, as they took some well-deserved downtime from all their work today, almost a belated date night but they never mentioned it. They sat on the deck of the yacht, while she served an incredibly lovely meal of fresh fish wrapped in some large native leaf, served with a lemon sauce. He was a hell of a cook himself, but she took his skills and completely turned them up a notch or ten.

"I may never cook again," he muttered, as he stared at the wonderful flambéed concoction in front of him.

She laughed. "I'm trying to impress you."

"Consider me impressed." He beamed at her. "But listen. You don't have to impress me. I've known you for years."

"Is that a good thing or a bad thing?" she asked. "It's almost like there's no excitement in a relationship if you've known somebody for years."

"But that's the basis for a more exciting relationship, as two people get closer. To start out with a sense of family, a sense of knowing already, is huge. It's the basics. It's the sharing of values before too many volatile emotions can lead us astray, without that good foundation. I'm not sure that having something that's calm and peaceful from the beginning isn't a nice thing in its own right, whether it leads to something greater or not."

"Sounds boring."

"Does it?" He looked at her in surprise, then frowned and thought about it. "I was thinking of it as more like a warm hug, something you could count on, somebody who you knew would be there in the tough times, not just the easy times."

She stared at him in surprise. "Oh, I like that. We've seen a lot, haven't we?"

"We have indeed, and tomorrow will bring a lot more people into our sphere, and that will change things again."

She leaned across and laced her fingers with his. "I've been enjoying our time together."

"It's almost sad to see it end, isn't it?" he murmured.

"It is. Maybe we should try to book some time at the island ourselves."

"I'm all for that," Dave said, with a laugh. "We'll have to fight everybody else to get here though."

She smiled. "Maybe. I guess it depends on what space there will be, as far as living quarters."

"I think it's likely to be pretty subdued with construction for a while. Bullard doesn't want to shock the environment or the nearby locals by moving in and taking over. Plus the whole point of a retreat is to give each of us some space, some solitude, some uninterrupted solace," he stated. "So whether there are ten huts here or fifteen, Bullard wants each one to be its own little hideaway. Then, if the team wants, they can come together for a group meal or a hike or a fishing trip or whatever. Everybody needs to heal. An awful lot of lingering trauma from all the different events that have gone on since that plane fell out of the sky."

"But it's over now, right?"

"Well, it is," he said, then hesitated. "I just don't know what's going on here."

"At least whoever it is hasn't tried anything new."

"No, and that's a good thing. I still suspect it's somebody from the mainland, and they're now afraid of getting caught."

"So, what was that? A really close warning shot?" she asked drily. "Because, honestly, it didn't feel like it."

"And that's a concern, isn't it?"

"It certainly is." She put on some gentle music, and they sat here on the deck of the yacht, enjoying their wine and the twinkle of the lights under the stars.

It really would all change tomorrow. Right now, it was just the three of them, but the captain was almost always off in his own quarters, where he visited over the satellite phone with his family, most evenings. He had two young children, and, while he didn't really like being away from them, this was the way he made a living.

"You want to dance?" Katie asked.

Dave looked at her in surprise. "Not sure I can." He motioned at his prosthetic.

She nodded. "Won't know until you try."

Awkwardly he got up and opened his arms. She stepped into them, and he wasn't sure that it was as much of a dance as it was a slow swaying to the music in the moonlight.

"Now this," she declared, "is romantic." He chuckled, the sound warm and gentle against her ear.

"That it is." He paused. "And tomorrow everything will change again."

"It doesn't have to," she said. "We've come together and made great progress between us. We don't have to slide backward."

"Everybody will be surprised if we act like we're a twosome," he noted.

"Does that matter?"

He thought about it, staring off into space, then shook his head. "No. It's probably better if everybody does know."

She leaned up and kissed him gently. "I'm all for that."

"You don't want to keep it quiet?"

"No, I really don't. I feel like we've wasted enough time."

"And here I was trying to be circumspect over you and your ex-husband."

"No need." Katie shook her head. "I dealt with that quite a while ago. He was a bully but only because he was so insecure inside. Those were his issues, and I've worked hard to recognize that and to leave it with him."

"Are you sure?"

She looked up at him and smiled. "Have you ever known me *not* to be sure about something?"

He grinned. "Okay. I was trying to be respectful."

"And I appreciate that, but I feel the need to share with you, as a woman, that you trying to be respectful is coming across as being really dense and slow." She smiled, waiting for his reaction.

He burst out laughing. "Well, I don't want you to think badly of me," he replied in a dry tone.

"Good." She looped her arms around his neck. "In that case, I suggest going one step further." And she reached up and kissed him gently on the chin.

Without hesitation, he lowered his head and kissed her softly on the lips.

She couldn't believe the tenderness, as if she were something breakable, something fragile. When he finally lifted his head, she murmured gently, "That was nice, but you know I'm not breakable, right?"

"No, but the moment is," he whispered. "Seems like a very long time since I held something so precious in my arms, and I don't want to ruin it." He kissed her gently, his hands stroking up and down her back.

Then she cuddled in closely, and they continued to move to the music.

He sighed. "I was thinking of this back at the compound, wondering if you'd be interested in going away for a holiday."

"And instead here we are in the beautiful South Pacific, enjoying a work trip." She raised her head to look up at him. "What could be better?"

"I hear you," he murmured, kissing her gently again.

Just then they heard footsteps, and the captain appeared. They broke apart. He took one look, raised an eyebrow, and smiled. "Well, I can see that love abounds, even out here. I approve heartily."

She flushed. "We've been friends for years."

"Friends make the best lovers," he stated, "because you already know who you are. You know that you don't have to worry about those things that really matter in a relationship, like values and honesty, because you've already worked that out."

"Ah, you're just one of those guys who loves to see a happy ending," she murmured.

"I am, indeed. Sorry to interrupt, but we've got company coming. I figured you would have noticed by now, but, considering you were otherwise engaged, I completely understand." He waggled his eyebrows.

She turned to look at Dave, but he'd already stepped away and searched the distance.

"What did you see?" Dave asked.

"A boat approaching," Sam replied, "but their lights are out. I was down below watching it, while I was talking to my daughter. When their running lights went out, I got suspicious and kept my eye on it. Now they're drifting." He pointed them out, and they were only about fifty meters off. "They're approaching now."

"With lights out and still moving toward us, as if under power," she murmured. "I'll take that as not a good sign."

"Nope, it's not a good sign at all. You should go down below," Dave said, walking over to the side of the yacht and opening a side panel. There he pulled out several handguns. As he reached for another one, he found her reaching for the small one in front.

"This is the one I prefer," she said calmly.

He looked at her and frowned.

She shook her head. "None of that. I won't let him attack you, while there's something I can do about it."

Dave opened his mouth to protest, when the captain called out, "Looks like we've got swimmers."

With that, Dave sat down close to the edge and moved to where he had a better view and was out of sight himself. They each quickly rearranged themselves flat along the dark edges, as Sam dropped down to the lowest level and set off to the other side. Dave knew that, if he didn't move, it would take the attackers time for their eyes to adjust.

Now he saw two swimmers. The fact that there was two of them was disturbing. There had been one shooter, but what they hadn't seen at the time was that a second person could have been with him. Yet Dave should have considered that. It would almost be expected, given most circumstances where any intruder would work with a partner. Clearly someone was after them.

As Dave watched, the slight foam of white water broke as a head surfaced. Dave studied him, wondering if the swimmers were bringing weapons on board. If they were, they would find a little more than they expected. Except that if they knew about the yacht, they should also know about the connections to Bullard and Leia. Were the intruders really prepared for that? Dave didn't think so. But then again, assholes full of arrogance were all over the world, so what were two more?

As Dave continued to watch, the two separated, one going left and one going right. The captain immediately joined him on the upper deck level and whispered, "I'll take this side."

Sam and Dave slipped back into position and waited, one of the swimmers approaching at the jumping-off landing water port, while the other pulled himself up to the front cabin area. Dave waited and watched as the first interloper came up silently and fully covered in a wet suit.

The first man turned, looked around, opened up his wetsuit, and withdrew a handgun with a silencer.

Immediately Dave knew he was dealing with a pro—or at least someone professional enough who had given him the wetsuit and the fancy silencer. He took steady aim and, with a single shot, took out the gunman's hand at the wrist. The man screamed and immediately dove back into the water. Maybe not the smartest move on his part, given that he would be pumping out blood that would attract predators.

But his handgun had dropped to the deck, and he was long gone under the water, probably heading back to the boat he'd come from. The man in the front of the yacht was dealing with the captain, and the two were in some kind of a fistfight, but the captain was six foot six and an easy three hundred pounds. He wasn't somebody you would take down fast. Dave went up to help him, and, coming up behind the second intruder, he put him in a little choke hold, until he lost his breath and dropped, unconscious.

At that point they dragged him over to where the other man had disappeared. "I shot him in the wrist," Dave told Sam, "and he dove back into the water."

"I wouldn't do that around here," Sam said. "I know we don't have a huge shark problem, but something like that will bring them in from miles around."

"I know. He might make it to his boat. It's not that far away."

"Well, this guy isn't going anywhere." The captain sneered, as he stared down at their captive.

The guy moaned and opened his eyes.

Dave looked down and smiled. "So, did today look like a good day to die?"

The man groaned again.

Dave looked at the captain. "Did he have a weapon?"

"I don't think so."

"I wonder if he was meant to be the decoy, while the other one came up and took care of us."

The man on the deck groaned. "Yeah, I didn't think you would go after him."

"We went after both of you. Why wouldn't we?" Dave snapped, as Katie slipped out of her hiding spot and joined them.

He groaned once more. "What did you do? It feels like you broke my jaw."

"Well, if I didn't, I'll try to next time. Who hired you?"

"The other guy. He thought he'd try one more time."

"One more time at what?"

"Cleaning up loose ends. He figured, if you guys were snooping around Leia's place, you're part of it."

"Part of what?" Dave asked. "We've got a ton more men coming in tomorrow, so, if you guys want to start playing games like that, you better be loaded for war."

"He won't like that at all."

"You're from the island?"

The man nodded. "Yes. And I didn't want to come out here, but he forced me to."

"And why is that?"

"Because I'm the one who told him about Leia being here."

"Ah, so he would kill us anyway. That's great," Dave noted. "But why did he want to?"

"Because there's still a price on Leia's head."

"Nope, that's been removed," Dave corrected.

The kid looked at him and shrugged. "Then I don't know. Maybe nobody told him."

"Maybe he'll be completely disinterested now that he's sporting a bullet in his wrist."

"I don't know about that. He was pretty adamant. He wanted Leia."

"And do I look anything like Leia?" Katie asked, exasperated. "I don't think so."

"Maybe not, but he heard rumors that she was coming back."

"So, you wanted to make sure that, if Leia did come back, he got to see her?"

"I'm not sure *getting to see her* is quite what he wanted," he admitted. "I think he was looking to take her himself."

"Ah, so it has nothing to do with that price on her head. It's more about the fact that he decided he should keep her?"

"Yes," the kid admitted. "That's when I realized I didn't want any part of it. She helped me. She's a good person. I feel miserable about it."

"You shouldn't have had any part of it anyway," Dave

snapped.

"When you think about it, and all she's done for you, the fact that you even started down this pathway is sad," Katie snapped. "Leia is coming back tomorrow. Imagine how she will feel when she hears about this."

He looked ashamed.

Good. He should. It was a shitty way to pay Leia back. Now all they had to do was catch the second asshole.

CHAPTER 5

NO DOUBT THAT the turn of events had changed the mood between Katie and Dave. Their prisoner was tied up securely and in a locked-up stateroom. Seemed Katie and Dave couldn't have one proper date. But she knew where they were headed now, and that was fine. It just wouldn't happen in the time frame she had hoped for. She had wanted that intimate time for themselves before they were descended upon by the rest of the team and the wedding guests. Intimate time to take the step to cement what Katie and Dave had. It would ease the uncertainty, before the others arrived and before life otherwise invaded their little private paradise.

She shook her head at that. It just wasn't to be. She was alone in her cabin right now. The captain was sleeping on deck, his preferred space when the weather was good, and Dave was in one of the other staterooms. She half wanted to get up and go to him but didn't really want to take the chance of getting rebuffed. It's not that they were in any imminent danger now, though there would always be some level of danger when involving a gunman on the loose, but, at the same time, she couldn't go to sleep because it just felt wrong.

When she heard a soft knock on her door, she quickly sat up. "Who is it?"

"It's me," Dave said.

She swung the blankets off her bed and walked to the door, opening it. "Is something wrong?"

He stared at her and winced. "Yes."

"What now?" she asked in horror.

He chuckled. "Nothing like that. I'm just …" And then he stopped, shrugged. "I'm missing you."

She looked at him in surprise and then looked deeper, seeing the uncertainty in his gaze and the need in his eyes that mirrored her own. Stepping back, she pulled the door open wider. "Then I suggest you come in," she said gently.

He looked at her and didn't move.

She shook her head. "Don't keep a lady waiting."

He smiled at that and stepped inside. No sooner had he closed the door, he had swept her into his arms and kissed her passionately.

She could feel her body lighting up with a fire she had kept banked for a very long time. This was what she'd hoped for, what she had desperately wanted, but what she had thought she wouldn't get.

And now that it was offered, freely, without any of the strings that she had been worried about earlier, she couldn't resist. She flung her arms around him and held him tight.

"I guess there's no point in asking if you're sure," he whispered.

"Don't insult me," she said. "Neither of us are in the first spring of youth, nor are we green. We've both been through relationships that put smiles on our faces and made us cry. This is where I want to be right now."

He smiled and lowered his head again.

She turned to move back to the bed. "And I'm also old enough to want the comfort of a bed."

He chuckled at that. "And yet you're so not old at all."

"No, maybe not," she agreed, "but there's definitely something to be said for comfort." At that, she flipped the covers back and laid down, so he could join her.

He slipped into the bed with her. "Do you think the captain will have a problem with this?"

"Are you kidding? He'll have a problem if we don't," she noted. "He's a romantic, like you wouldn't believe."

He chuckled and pulled her snugly into his arms. "I wanted this earlier, but everything changed all at once there."

"I know," she murmured. "And that was tough in its own way. I was just lying here, thinking about that too."

He nuzzled her neck up to her ear, making her toes quiver and her belly tighten.

She smiled as she wrapped her arms tighter around him and giggled as he tickled her, then laughed as his hand stroked across her skin under her short T-shirt. "I forgot to tell you that I'm ticklish."

"That's okay," he murmured, his warm breath brushing along her cheek and neck. "I'm pretty sure we'll get you past it eventually, with much practice."

At that, she burst out laughing. Soon the laughter turned to moans, as he cradled her soft curves. She twisted as his hand slid down to cup the cheek of her buttocks, then slid around to her thigh, all the way down her calf to her foot. She twisted in his arms, loving the slow exploration, at the same time realizing there really was no rush. It was another advantage of their age and circumstances. No need to push and to drive this forward. They had the luxury of time to savor and to enjoy it, the way they'd always hoped.

His touch was soft and soothing, yet intimate, awakening nerve endings that she hadn't deliberately shut off but had become pickier about after she had broken off her marriage and then finally began testing the dating waters. It had been a long time for her, and, as Dave gently raised the temperature in the room, she realized how much she had missed this, and how much she loved being held and caressed. Nothing else could replace having that one special person who wanted to be with her.

She moaned, as he built up the tempo of his strokes and his kisses. She could feel his heartbeat racing under her hand, as she tried to explore for equal time, but she could sense that his needs were rising at a pace faster than hers. She tried to slow him down, but he shivered with need. She looked up at him and smiled. "It's okay, you know, if you get there faster than I do."

He shook his head. "No, it's not. I want us to get there together." He lowered his head to one plump breast, took her nipple into his mouth, and suckled deeply. She arched her back and cried out, as he suckled hard for several long seconds, then moved to the other one. She caressed his head, her fingers sliding through his hair, as he slowly worked his way down to her ribs, her navel, her hip bones, then to her hollow in between.

By the time he found her center with his tongue and suckled gently, she was already climbing off the bed, trying to pull him onto her. He slowly made his way back up again, but his fingers were busy in the damp curls at the apex of her thighs, and she was shuddering, slowly losing her mind, when he finally eased himself to her opening.

She wrapped her thighs around his hips and whispered, "Welcome home."

And he slowly drove in deep and seated himself at the heart of her. She moaned, shifting gently, trying to adjust to the size of him, and then he started to move.

Slowly he built up the pressure, his fingers sliding into the hair behind her ears, holding her head firm, while he kissed her, driving them faster and faster. She could only hang on for the ride, already having lost all sense of control of her body, as her own needs rose up, fast and furious.

When he threw them both off the cliff, she felt her body splinter into a thousand pieces, as she listened to his roar above her. He crashed down beside her and cuddled her close. "Now that," he whispered, "is something I've been desperately wanting—for a very long time."

She was still gasping for air, her heart pounding, racing against her chest. "You could have made a move a couple years ago."

"Well, I would have, but you picked up with that new boyfriend, so I backed off again."

"And I picked up with that new boyfriend because I was trying to get you to make a move."

He rolled over and looked at her. "Really?"

"Yes." She laughed. "Really."

"Maybe I am a little dense," he said. "You have to make things very clear to me."

She leaned up, kissed him gently. "Is that clear enough?"

"Definitely." He collapsed beside her again, tucking her up even closer. "But we still need to get some sleep. No telling what tomorrow will bring."

"Sleep we can do," she murmured, nuzzling against him. "We can always wake up and have a repeat."

He chuckled, and she closed her eyes and fell asleep in his arms.

WAKING UP THE next morning, Dave found Katie, her arms wrapped around him, her head resting on his chest, but her fingers moving in a repetitive pattern on his arm, as if her mind were going one million miles an hour, working out the logistics of something.

He cuddled her close and dropped a kiss on her forehead. "Good morning to you too."

She smiled, lifted her head, and kissed him gently on the lips. "Good morning. I tend to be an early riser. At the moment it looks like my mind is caught up in a huge To-Do list of what I need to get to from this point forward."

"We definitely need to get going on some things. Are you ready to get up?"

"Not really, but considering it's already nine o'clock, I'd better."

He looked at her in surprise.

She nodded. "We did avoid sleeping as much as we could last night, apparently."

"I don't think we avoided anything," he said, with a smile. "I think it was more a case of enjoying having something to do other than sleep."

"Well, that's one way to put it." She chuckled, then sat up, completely unselfconscious of her nudity, swinging her legs over the side of the bed. Walking over to grab a change of clothes, she dressed quickly into a two-piece bathing suit, with a flowing dress atop it. "I'm going for a swim. You'll join me?"

"Absolutely. Give me a second. I've got to find something to swim in."

"I'm totally okay if you go like that." Katie motioned at his bare body.

"Ha! I generally don't go swimming nude because my

prosthetic tends to scare people."

She looked at it, shrugged. "It is what it is. If you get dressed and come join me, I'll put on the coffee. We can have it on the deck, after our swim." Then she left him to his own devices.

He went back to his room, quickly got changed into his swim trunks, and grabbing a T-shirt, headed up after her.

The captain was on the deck, talking on the satellite phone. He lifted a hand when he saw them and muttered, "Most of us keep working hours." Yet he sported a big grin.

"Thank you for that." Dave sat down beside him. "Any news?"

"Outside of the fact that everybody's on their way, no."

"Well, I take that as a good sign. How about our prisoner?"

"I checked him a couple times during the night. He's doing fine."

"That's good. I hope the guys are planning on taking him away from here."

"I think they're planning on talking to him first."

"Good," Dave said, "as long as it's not my job."

"Ha! Getting soft in your old age."

"Maybe," he admitted. "And certainly turning my attention to other things." He glanced back into the kitchen area.

The captain laughed uproariously. "You two are good together. She's been waiting for this for a long time."

"Apparently she finds me slow and incredibly dense on some topics," Dave said on a laugh.

"Yeah, I knew that. But, hey, you finally got there."

"I guess I was being too much of a gentleman," he muttered.

"And she was going too easy, thinking that you needed

more time to get over your losses."

"That was a long time ago." His voice was soft and gentle, as he remembered his wife and daughter. Both of them gone now by many years.

"Well, like I said, maybe it's a good time."

"When are the guys getting here?"

"Sooner than I thought," Sam noted. "I suspect we'll have a few of them here in a couple hours."

"They didn't give you an ETA?"

"Check your phone," Sam said. "I think they've been trying to get hold of you."

Dave nodded. "I turned off my phone."

"Smart man." The captain smirked.

Just then Katie came out with a tray laden with coffee.

The captain looked at it and smiled. "See now? That was worth waiting for. I've been waiting for you guys to get your asses out of bed."

"Any other day ..." Dave stood, pulling off his T-shirt over his head. "I was *especially* tired."

At that, she laughed and, tossing the blue flowing dress off her shoulders, walked to the edge and jumped into the water. Dave, after removing his prosthetic, was just a few seconds behind her.

The captain grabbed one of the coffee cups, enjoying the moment, as he stood at the railing, his big voice booming out. "It's a beautiful day, and this is definitely the place to enjoy paradise."

"And, if it weren't for the prisoner and a gunman on the loose, it would be." Katie rolled over, her head back, floating gently in the water.

Dave twisted and rolled, generally just having a great time, feeling the cold water on his skin. It felt refreshing and clean, and today he felt like a whole new man, in a way. He'd forgotten about the prisoner, until he woke up. And that was very unusual for him, and it also showed where he might be heading in life right now, which was allowing for other things to occupy his mind.

He glanced at Katie, and she gave him a special smile, leaned over, kissed him gently. "Breakfast?"

"Only if you're ready to go in," he said.

"I can't believe we're here as it is. Why doesn't Bullard just move his base operations here?" she asked. "Just look at how it would be. We'd have a great time."

"Now that he's getting married, he probably won't do anywhere near the traveling he used to do," Dave guessed.

She nodded. "Which means I may end up looking for a new job?"

"I hope not," he said.

She looked at him in surprise.

He shrugged. "I'd hate to lose you."

"I wasn't planning on going anywhere—outside of somebody else's kitchen, temporarily."

He nodded, realizing that she would probably travel more than he would now. His job was generally at the compound these days. He'd traveled more in the last four months, chasing leads looking for Bullard, than he had in years. And now he was starting a relationship with Katie, somebody who could end up traveling far away from him.

It was something he'd have to deal with. But he wouldn't dare choke up about it because that was a sure-fire way of making her feel like she had no space. And he wasn't up for that. He'd do a hell of a lot to keep her in his life right now. She was a very special woman.

He smiled. "Breakfast sounds great." He looked at her.

"You want me to cook?"

She rolled over onto her back again. "Sure, if you want to. I certainly don't have to cook every meal just because it's my job."

"Plus, you'll get busier with everybody headed this way," he murmured. "But maybe we'll do that in a few minutes, since this is pretty great as it is." The two of them floated gently on the ocean, and he couldn't find anything to dampen his mood. At this moment, things were pretty damn perfect.

CHAPTER 6

K ATIE ROLLED OVER with a sad sigh. "Come on. Breakfast time. I don't know about you, but I've got to get moving."

Up on the deck she quickly put on the blue dress and headed down to the kitchen. She quickly whipped up eggs benedict with some smoked salmon on the side, with a little bit of greens, and carried it up for the three of them.

As she arrived, both men were on their phones, both looking very serious. She immediately realized something was up. She set up the food on the trolley and poured coffee for everybody, then sat down with hers, waiting quietly for them to tell her what was going on.

When Dave finally got off the phone, he looked at the breakfast, then smiled. "Ah, you cooked. This looks delicious."

"I ended up making it. Sorry, I completely forgot about your offer. Force of habit, I guess."

"There's time for me to cook other breakfasts," he noted. "I'm a decent hand in the kitchen, but I'm certainly not a professional chef."

"A lot of good cooks out there never had any training."

"Maybe. I think I'm probably one of them."

She smiled. "It would be nice if we shared a passion for cooking."

"Absolutely."

"So, enough of that. What the hell is going on?" She motioned at Dave and the captain, who was still busy on the sat phone. "Are there problems?"

"A couple connecting planes got missed, due to delays at an airport," he explained. "The usual logistics of moving that many people. The guys will be here soon though."

"And our prisoner?"

"I think they're planning on having a serious talk with him, then probably letting him go."

"Interesting," she murmured.

"Are you okay with that?"

"I'm okay with that," she acknowledged. "I'd rather that than giving him a beat down, especially if he is someone Leia has tried to help."

"It's the other guy we want," Dave said, "but, with the boat gone, it might be a little harder to find him."

"Have you checked the hospitals on the mainland?"

"Yep. The word is out, so it's just a matter of time to figure out where else he could have gone."

"If Leia were here, she would be the logical choice. But she's not here."

"So, in other words, the old medicine woman?"

"I would think it would be worth checking out anyway."

He nodded. "We'll take a walk around to her later."

"You don't think she'll tell you?"

"I don't know. I think the islanders are fairly tight."

"Is there anything to worry about?"

"I hope not," he said.

They finished breakfast quickly, and then Katie stood. "I want to go back to Leia's place, so I can take a better look and take some more measurements." She held up a pad of paper and a tape measure, ready to get down to business.

"Good enough," Dave said. "Let's go."

As they got into the small skiff to make their way to the island, she noticed he was well armed. "Are you expecting trouble?" she asked quietly.

"Expecting trouble, no. Ready for it, yes. I got caught by surprise yesterday, and that's not happening again."

She nodded. "Is it okay to leave the captain alone with the prisoner?"

"He's fully armed," he said confidently. "I don't think that kid wants to tangle with him. Honestly, I don't think that kid wants a part of any of it."

She didn't say anything because there was absolutely nothing to say. They were short on men, and she really needed to take another look at the venue, so she could be well prepared to feed a large crew.

As soon as they landed, they tied up in the usual spot, realizing that part of what she needed to do was figure out how they would get items off the small skiff onto land. "We'll need a better transport system here for sure."

"Once the men get here," Dave added, "they'll be bringing and pulling together parts of a floating dock immediately."

"Are some coming by boat then?"

"They are," he confirmed.

She left it at that, and, before long, they were measuring and discussing options. "So we can get a maximum of ten of our folding tables up here." She thought about what all she needed. "That would leave one spare."

"If you can get away with nine, we'd be better off," Dave noted, "because we've got to have room for people to walk around."

"I guess it depends on how quickly we can get something of a platform or a deck made here," she murmured.

"There will be a ton of building going on as soon as the team gets here, but you'll see that within a few hours."

"I hope so," she said, "because, at the moment, it just seems like an idyllic holiday mixed in with moments of terror."

He looked at her and smiled. "Oh, I hope those parts with me aren't idyllic terror."

She burst out laughing. "Absolutely not, but what a great way to look at it."

"I don't think so," he protested. But he was smiling, and generally he felt just a sense of peace in his heart that he hadn't felt for a very long time.

The good news was that she didn't feel like she was part of the equation where the trouble was concerned. Whoever it was who had shot at them before had apparently been after Leia, not Katie, so she was happy to let Dave look after that problem.

By the time they were finished with their plans, and she'd wandered up and around again, trying to figure out how much of Leia's space they could make use of, she turned to Dave. "It's really hard to finalize plans until we know what access we'll have here."

"I know," he said. "That's all part of the larger scheme too."

"So, isn't this wedding rushing it a bit?"

"It is, but it's also where Leia needs to come back and say goodbye."

"Right." Katie could understand that. She herself had spent a lot of years working at this crazy job, traveling all over the world, and hadn't put roots down anywhere. She had always been totally open to just going wherever she needed to be. "I guess I can understand that," she said. "I don't really have much in the way of a home base anywhere to say goodbye to."

"And are you okay with that?" Dave asked. "You always are there and available for work, so I never stopped to think if you had a permanent home somewhere."

"Right." She laughed. "I *am* a workaholic. Don't worry. I feel at home when I'm with you."

He grinned at that. "Did you ever want to get married again?" he asked her. "Or were you planning on being a jet-setting career woman all your life?"

"At one point in time, I was hoping for a family. But I'm not sure that'll happen now."

"Why is that?"

"I never met anybody up to it, until now," she said, "and I'm not sure what your thoughts are."

He looked at her in surprise and then down at his hands. "I would like to have a family at some point," he murmured. "It would really help fill that lingering need inside."

"I'm sorry about what happened to yours."

"So am I, but it was a long time ago, and I'm as over it as I'm likely to get, I think. I will never forget either of them, of course, but I would never advocate for someone in that situation to stop living."

"Good. So, two or three?" He looked at her blankly, and quickly she grinned, realizing again that she needed to be more specific. "Two kids or three?"

He burst out laughing. "How about we start with one?"

"GOOD." KATIE GRINNED. "Because ... you remember last

night?"

He looked at her quizzically. "Definitely. How could I forget?"

"I wasn't prepared for that to happen, and I didn't use any birth control."

He could feel something inside his heart stop, then stared at her in shock. "Wow. Way to hit me where it counts."

"Just a warning. After all that happened yesterday, it's not like we were thinking all that clearly, right?"

"No, that's for sure," he said. "But, if it happens, I can't say I'd be at all upset."

"Neither would I."

With that, he helped her back into the skiff, and they headed around the point toward the village again. This time they drew less attention, but they were standing closer together this visit, and, instead of just holding hands, she had her arm looped through his elbow.

"So we don't appear to be quite the oddity today that we were yesterday," she noted quietly.

"No, I noticed that. I'll take that as a good thing."

"I'd say so," she murmured. "It's interesting how quickly we get used to a different norm."

"Looks like Leia led the way for a lot of them."

"True enough."

As they walked up to the old medicine woman's home, a line was waiting to see her. Dave stepped forward and asked, "Is there a problem here? What's going on?"

"She was attacked," said one of the men, his voice harsh.

Dave stared at him in shock. "When?" he asked urgently.

"Yesterday."

At that, Dave stepped around the line to try to see the

woman herself. And, indeed, she was unconscious and sported a head wound. He bent down to look at it from a Western medicine point of view. "It doesn't look very good," he muttered. "That is pretty serious, as far as head trauma goes."

"Where's Leia?" one of the men asked. "She would fix this."

"I don't know if she can fix this. It probably needs time as much as anything." Dave gently checked the bloody area covering the old woman's hair. He found an open wound that needed stitching. "We need to close this wound." He pulled out his phone and sent Bullard a message, asking for a time frame for his arrival.

Instead of getting a text response, his phone rang. *Bullard.*

"We're on our way. Maybe two hours."

"Is Leia there?"

"Yes, why?"

"Let me talk to her."

Bullard immediately handed over the phone.

"Leia, the old medicine woman has been attacked."

"Oh my God. "How badly?"

"She's got an open head wound. The wound itself isn't that bad," he noted. "The trauma will be the problem. I can certainly stitch it up, though it's a day late."

"That would have been better of course. But still, it will heal faster with less chance of infection if you can clean it up now and close the wound."

"Did you leave any medical supplies here?" he asked.

"Yes, she has some there," Leia said quietly. "Send me a photo of the injuries."

He quickly disconnected and sent photos, then spoke to one of the women nearby. "Leia left some medical supplies.

Do you know where they are?"

She looked at him blankly. One of the other men translated, and she immediately got up, walked over, and pulled out a large basket, carrying it to him.

He riffled through it to find disinfectant, antibiotic lotion, some sutures, and even casting material to set broken bones. He smiled at that and immediately cleaned the woman's head, while she lay here unconscious, then quickly sutured up the wound on the one side. He was checking over the rest of her, when his phone rang.

Katie answered it for him. "Leia wants to know if there are any other injuries?"

He shook his head. "Not that I can see. It looks like she was attacked from behind."

After she relayed that, Katie turned back to Dave. "Leia said there's no violence on the island."

"She doesn't know about the potshot somebody took at us or the guy on the boat that we've got tied up." He turned to look at the others. "Did anybody see anything?" Dave counted several headshakes, but one man stood there, staring at him. "What did you see?" Dave asked.

The man shrugged. "One of you."

"One of us? A white man?"

"Yes. He came here for help."

"Did he have an injured wrist?" He pointed above his hand.

The man nodded. "It was bandaged. He asked her for help."

"And she wouldn't give it?"

He shook his head. "She said she couldn't help him. He got really angry and hit her."

"*Nice*," he muttered. "I wonder why she wouldn't help him?"

"It was ugly," said one of the women. "The hand, it was an ugly wound."

Dave nodded. It should have been because he's the one who created it. He looked around. "Does anybody here know who he was?"

They looked at each other, but nobody said a word.

He sighed. "Come on, guys. I know he's been around here. But we need to help her, and I need to know who did this."

They just shook their heads and wouldn't say a word.

He looked at Katie and shrugged. "Any ideas?"

She held out the phone, with Leia still on the call, speaking to one of the young women.

"Leia wants to ask some questions."

The woman took the phone. "Leia?"

The conversation was one-sided, as they couldn't hear the rest of it, but the woman fell silent after being animated, and then she gave a name.

When the phone was handed back to her, Katie asked, "What was that all about?"

"One of the old woman's family did this," she said.

Katie shook her head. "Ouch. Pretty harsh to do this to your own family. Especially to someone her age."

"If she wouldn't help him, I can see it," Leia explained, her voice harsh. "He's always been a problem. He always wants more than he has."

"But I thought he was white."

"Yes, and he only comes here when he wants something. His father was a white man. His mother was a native woman from the island. His mother went with his father to the mainland and then came back many years later with a son. It's Pietro and his friend Ramon."

CHAPTER 7

KATIE COULD SEE the consternation among the faces in the group, when the locals realized they knew who had attacked the old woman, and that it was a black sheep of her own family. Katie looked down, as Dave gently made the older woman more comfortable, straightening up her body and placing a pillow ever-so-slightly under her neck to support it before covering her up. She checked for a temperature, as his gaze studied her skin.

"You have a lot of medical experience, don't you?" Katie asked Dave.

"Bullard and I both do," he said.

"Will she be okay?" one of the women asked anxiously. The woman was heavy with child, and it was obvious that she was close to her time and stressed out.

He turned toward her. "I can't be sure. She'll need to wake up for us to evaluate that."

The woman nodded and gently rubbed her belly. "I need her to help with the baby," she murmured.

"Does she look after everybody's medical needs here?"

The group nodded.

He frowned at that. "Do you not go to the mainland at all?"

"Not if we can help it," the woman said. "We have to pay them."

"And here, she just looks after you?"

"We've come to her for decades, generations even," the woman explained.

He nodded and assessed the look of his unconscious patient again.

"You're not happy about how she looks, are you?" Katie asked.

"I'd feel a lot better if she were awake. Concussions are tricky things, and so are head wounds."

Katie didn't know the first thing about that kind of medicine. "Well, Leia's coming. Maybe she'll help."

"She might, and she'll certainly settle down these other people, I'll bet, but there's nothing much to be done for head injuries like this. It just takes time."

"If the old woman were in a hospital, would she be okay?"

"Only if the brain isn't swelling inside," he noted. "They would just monitor her otherwise. And it's like they say, medical care is out of reach for anybody here. There's no free medical anywhere, and they don't have a way to earn cash."

"Right." Katie sighed at that. "Life is just fine and dandy, until something traumatizing happens, and then you realize the safety net you thought you had isn't quite a safety net anymore."

He nodded and stepped up to some of the locals. "Where can we find this Pietro?"

One of the men shrugged. "He went back to the mainland."

"To get his wrist fixed?"

One of the other men said, "To bring back friends."

"Ah, so, he wants to continue the fight, huh?"

The other man nodded.

"We'll see how he likes that," Dave muttered. "And what about Ramon?"

"We haven't seen him," one of the women said nervously. "Not since yesterday."

"Does he hang around with Pietro a lot?"

"Too much," the man replied.

"And what about anybody else here? Do they hang out with that group?"

"No," the pregnant woman replied. "Most of us just want to live our peaceful island life."

"And Pietro and Ramon want something different?"

"They always want something different," she said, stifling a heavy groan, as she tried to shift the large weight she was carrying.

Katie looked at her. "Is it just one baby or two?" she asked, with a smile.

"One. I think." She gave her a bright smile. "But I'm overdue."

"Ah, so that will be fun too," Dave said, as he studied her. "You're in labor, aren't you?"

She looked at him fearfully. "How did you know?" she asked.

"I recognize the signs."

"Are you a doctor?" she asked hopefully.

"Not like a midwife, no," he said. "But I've done a lot of doctoring in my time." He looked at his watch. "Leia should be here in about an hour and a half." That brought a murmur of excitement from the others. "Does anybody resent Leia being here?" he asked.

Immediately everybody shook their heads. "No. She saved many of us," the pregnant woman said. "She helped my sister deliver her baby, and we thought it was dead. But

Leia saved it."

"Well, let's hope she arrives in time to help you with your birth," Dave said quietly. He looked back at Katie. "We need to head back."

She nodded. "I don't feel very good about leaving the medicine woman."

"We'll stay with her," the pregnant woman said. "Can we send you word if something changes?"

"Please do, and, as soon as we see Leia, we'll bring her here."

At that, everybody seemed to calm down slightly. Dave and Katie represented a new element here, but Leia's good relationship with them was giving them access to the group of villagers. Although Pietro targeting Leia had brought the trouble here too.

With that, Dave smiled, turned, and reached out a hand for Katie, and they slowly walked back to their boat.

"Do you think it's safe to leave?"

"We have to. And the villagers need to figure out what Pietro and Ramon are doing here as well."

She grimaced. "I'm not sure they have a clue. Obviously some relatives in every family don't like the scenario, and I think that's what we've got going on here."

"I wonder if it was Leia as a woman or Leia as a doctor who was valuable to them."

"Kind of sucks if it's either slash or. But considering how poor their medical service is, I'm guessing it may be the doctor part."

"It's not so much that it's poor medical help just because their lives are simple. I'm sure the medicine woman has picked up many natural tricks over the years to heal people. Sometimes we just complicate things with our modern

Western medicine," he murmured.

"But I don't think they're quite ready to let go of Leia's magic or their medicine woman's skills," Katie noted.

"No, definitely not." Dave turned to help Katie into the skiff. He looked back to see everybody watching, as if they had followed them down to the water. "I'm not sure when they came after us. I didn't see them, did you?"

She shrugged. "I wasn't really watching, but I saw them, yes."

He smiled at them and helped her into the boat, then slowly pulled out.

"Times are changing here, aren't they?" she asked quietly.

"Time changes everywhere," he noted in an equally quiet voice.

"I can't imagine living a life like this."

"More joy. Maybe more hardship too sometimes, but it's a simpler life that isn't so driven all the time. It's a lot more peaceful."

"Until you have something like these young men, seeking something more."

"Very true." At that, Dave and Katie stayed quiet, and they drifted, slowly motoring their way back toward the yacht.

When they got on board, she called out to the captain, "Are you ready for food?" When she got no answer, she turned and headed to the kitchen. But there was no sign of him there. She ran upstairs and called out again. "Where is he?"

His face grim, Dave came back from searching the pilot area. "No clue. The prisoner is gone too."

She froze at that. "Oh my God. Do you think they took

Sam too?"

"Worse would be if they deep-sixed him."

Her heart quaked at that idea because the captain was a hell of a good man and such a dedicated husband and father. There was nothing more important than the family he held so close.

They quickly raced around on the second deck, and, under one of the lifeboats, Dave stopped and pointed to a bit of fabric sticking out. With a handgun at the ready, he quickly lifted a corner and snapped, "Hands up!"

The captain cut loose with a roar. Easing up the end of the lifeboat, Dave found Sam lying there, tied up, furious, and gagged.

Dave immediately holstered his pistol and helped the captain out from underneath the lifeboat, so they could get him untied. As the captain sat up, he swore. "I know I've got a harder head than most, but I really don't like getting it smashed."

Immediately Dave took a look at his head; they had broken the skin when they had knocked him out. "On the other hand, it's a damn good thing they only knocked you out."

"If you say so. I can't say I see a single good thing about any of this," he snapped.

"How many were there?"

"No clue. I didn't see anything. I was studying the maps and looking at the weather charts, when this guy came up behind me. I turned and got hit over the head."

"Sorry about that." Dave helped the captain up to the deck, where he sat him back down.

Katie immediately brought some water for him. "We really do need backup now," she said.

"I've already called it in," Dave replied gently. "They

will be here soon."

She walked over to him, and he immediately opened his arms and gave her a hug. "It'll be fine," he murmured.

"Maybe, and maybe not. I'm sure seeing the uglier side of your work."

"True. But something like this could happen anywhere."

"I guess. I just don't like to see it."

"None of us do," he replied, with a gentle smile. He dropped a kiss on her forehead. "What about lunch?"

"Can you eat right now?"

"Absolutely. Plus, it might help the captain feel better."

She went to the galley area and quickly made up some sandwiches that she brought out.

The captain's eyes lit up when he saw the food. "Nothing like food to make you feel better."

"If it had been me hit over the head," she said, "it would be all I could do to get any food down at all."

"That's because you're a girl, with a softer head." Sam munched down on the first sandwich he could reach. "My head's pretty hard. It's just my temper that's the problem right now. I can't believe the little buggers snuck up on me."

"You had your headset on, didn't you?"

He looked at her, shamefaced. "I did. I was listening to some of the songs my son wanted me to hear." Then he shrugged. "Can't say it was worth getting hit over the head about either."

She chuckled at that. "It's all good. I won't tattle on you."

He rolled his eyes. "Somebody needs to because there has to be an explanation for why I got hit."

"Your guard was down," she said. "We're all experiencing something similar."

"We're not supposed to though," Sam complained. "Obviously things are very off here."

She added, "I think it's just off for these two young punks."

Just then, Dave's phone beeped, with a text message. He looked down at it, smiled, and said, "Guess what?"

"What?" the captain asked in a testy voice.

"Looks like we're about to get company. Good company this time."

DAVE LOOKED UP to see a speedboat coming toward them. He lifted a hand in greeting, as they approached. And, sure enough, there was Bullard, Leia, Fallon, and Linny too—Fallon's partner and Dave's niece. Dave smiled. "Well, here's four out of at least twelve?"

"At least." Fallon gave a jovial laugh, as he hopped on board, helping Linny next, and took one look at the captain, and frowned. "What the hell?"

"Don't even start," the captain groused.

Dave hugged his niece, happy to see her so happy.

"You really got hit from behind?" Fallon asked Sam.

He pointed to the head wound, and there was no mistaking that, from the angle of the blow, he'd been taken down from behind.

"So, even in paradise, there's still a little hell."

"We were hoping that it was all dealt with," Dave said, looking at Leia and smiling. "But your paradise has a few vipers."

"Every paradise does." Then her face twisted, as she worried about the island and its people. "How is the wise old one?"

"Not so good. Also a very pregnant woman really hopes she'll get back on her feet fast."

"That's Micla. I guess she's due now, isn't she?"

"She looks like she was due weeks ago," Dave confirmed. "I don't know if you can willfully hold a child in, but, if she gets her choice, she won't let that birth happen until the old woman can help her."

"That's not a great idea either." Leia looked up at Bullard. "I better get over there."

Bullard nodded. "I'm coming too."

She smiled. "They won't hurt me."

"I'm coming," Bullard said in a firm voice.

She raised both hands in frustration. "Fine, be protective then."

"I intend to," he stated, with a cheeky grin.

Dave said, "Maybe I'll come along with you, as long as Fallon and Linny are good to stay with Captain Sam and Katie."

With everyone in agreement, they headed to the small skiff, and Dave slowly motored them around the island to the village.

"I always walk," Leia said. "I don't ever come this way."

"There was no need to before," Bullard said quietly. "Why would you get into a rowboat that will be hard to navigate in the ocean waters, especially when high winds come up, if you can just walk?"

She just smiled at him and his island ways. As she got off the skiff and onto the dock, several people raced toward her. Lots of hugs and exclamations and greetings were exchanged all around. Then, almost as one, the entourage, the entire troop, headed toward the old medicine woman. As they got closer, more and more people joined in.

"Wow," Dave said to Bullard. "Leia really is loved here. Her and the medicine woman."

Bullard nodded. "It's causing me a little bit of trouble too, as far as keeping Leia happy in Africa."

"Well, I can see that she will want to come back on a regular basis. These people have become like family to her."

"And a family who accepted her," Bullard stated.

"All the more reason," Dave said. "We all know what that's like."

"I understand, but I don't know that I want to lose her that often."

"Well, like Katie said, maybe you need to make this another stronghold."

Bullard looked at him and started to laugh. "I don't think anybody will get any work done while they're here."

"And maybe that's a good thing too," Dave replied. "Everybody works too much as it is."

"So many new relationships are developing right now," Bullard noted. "I'm half afraid nobody will ever work again." He turned to Dave. "You included."

Dave looked at him in surprise, then realized what he meant and flushed. "Hey, Katie and I have been heading in that direction for a long time."

"And I'm damn glad to see it," he said. "I've thought a couple times that I might have to do something to throw you two together, but it looks like you finally got there on your own."

Dave smiled. "Absolutely. Absolutely."

"But how serious is it?"

"She asked me how many kids I wanted today," he mentioned sheepishly.

Bullard looked at him and started to laugh. "Well, in

that case, it's damn serious. She's been after a family for a long time."

"Yeah. I'm both excited and terrified."

"With good reason," he admitted. "You lost everything, man. Now you've been given a second chance. I would take it, if I were you."

"I'm planning on it," Dave added. "All the excitement on this trip has brought us closer, that's for sure."

"Sorry for the trouble, but I'm really glad for you, Dave."

"Thanks. It sure changes how you look at things." He turned his attention back to see the old woman, stretched out just as he'd left her. She didn't show any signs of having moved at all. He frowned at that. "She's in exactly the same position as I left her in."

"Yes, of course," Leia said, with a heavy sigh. "She's *well past her end date*."

"What?" he asked, not sure he'd actually heard her say that.

Leia smiled. "We used to joke about it, the two of us. We think she's well in her nineties."

"Much harder to recover from something like this then."

"She was also ready to go, but looking for somebody who would help take over the island and her position. But she never found anybody who had quite the right qualifications and personality."

"Understood, and that's got to be tough."

"It is. She spent her lifetime looking for somebody to help."

"Which is another reason you bonded with her so well. If you had been a local, her search would have ended."

"Yes. But it's also not my place, not my home. I'm happy to be a visitor and a regular tourist," she admitted. "But it's a whole different story to devote your life to looking after a village like this."

"Maybe they'll have to make more trips to the mainland," Dave suggested.

"And it also depends on how often we'll come back," Bullard said.

Leia looked up at him and smiled knowingly. "You don't want to come back at all."

"That's not true," he protested. "I just want to make sure you're safe."

"You can't keep me all bundled up forever," she murmured.

"But I can try," he said.

She just shook her head, but her happy smile was evident.

Just then there was a movement from the old woman on the floor. As she opened her eyes slowly, to see everybody around her staring, her gaze landed on Leia. She smiled immediately and reached out a hand.

Leia grabbed her hand and just held it close to her heart, then spoke some interesting words that nobody really understood.

Dave looked at Bullard, but Bullard was trying to figure it out himself.

Finally Leia settled back. "She will pull through this time," she stated, looking around at the others. "But, as I've told you many times, her time is coming. She doesn't have much more to give."

"But you didn't give us a time," the pregnant woman said.

"Nobody can give you a time," she corrected. "When it's

time for her to go, she'll go."

There was sadness in everybody's face but also joy that the medicine woman would make it through this time.

Leia stood again and eased the medicine woman out of the awkward position she'd been in. She looked at Bullard. "They will likely have to do more and more trips to the mainland, and there is a trend toward that, but there's also a lot of people who don't want anything to do with it. There's a monetary system on the island that doesn't really work well for them here."

"No, of course not," Bullard said. "Is there free care for anybody?"

"No, not free, at least I don't think so. But there is a bartering system that a lot of them employ."

"That's good at least." Bullard just shook his head, as the others surrounded them, with several trying to talk to Leia.

She listened to several, gave advice to a couple, and then her gaze landed on the very heavily pregnant woman standing off to the side. She frowned and walked over. "You need to lie down."

The young woman stared at her defiantly.

"She will live, but she may not be of any use for your birth at this time," she said quietly.

"I was waiting for somebody to help. Are you staying long enough to be here?"

"If you would relax and allow that child to be born, we'll have this over and done with in just a few hours."

The young woman flashed a bright smile. "In that case, I will go lie down."

"But you need to be calm because that baby is bound and determined to come now." And, with that, Leia turned to Bullard, "I'll go help deliver her child."

"Right now?"

"Yes, right now."

Bullard looked at Dave, who shrugged. "I'll head back to the launch. Obviously you're staying here with Leia."

"Obviously," Bullard said, with a grin.

"Hey," Leia said, "you'd be just as bad. I've seen you deliver babies in the clinic yourself."

"Sure, but I had a full set of equipment."

"Well, you get to learn new ways here," Leia replied, with a smirk. "And, if everything goes well, it's fine. When there's no equipment and when we have big problems, then it's a huge issue."

"How long to the mainland?"

"Over an hour, and that's only in ideal weather conditions."

"Big cities sometimes have to wait that long to get an ambulance anyway," he muttered.

She nodded. "Unfortunately that's very true." And she and the pregnant woman disappeared into a small hut off to the side.

Dave reached up, slapped Bullard on the shoulder. "Have fun."

"Great. If I need an assistant ..." Bullard let his words trail off.

"You *are* the assistant this time," Dave said, with a big grin.

"That I am. That I am." With a deep breath, Bullard headed toward the small hut and poked his head in. He spoke with Leia for a few minutes, then popped out. "Dave, we'll be fine here. Maybe come back in an hour or two."

"Will do." Dave returned to the skiff.

What he needed to do first was figure out where the

pathways were so they could make that walk. By the time he got to Leia's corner, it would be almost time to turn around and check back with Bullard again.

As he made it to where Leia's little corner was, he saw Fallon and Linny walking around the space, getting acclimated. He docked, hopped out of the boat, and saw Katie there too, once again with her tape measure. He smiled at her and said, "The old woman woke up, seems to be coherent. Leia is staying to help deliver the pregnant woman's baby, and Bullard is staying to look after Leia."

Katie grinned at that. "That's perfect. The circle of life and all. It's a cycle of life and death."

"Let's hope there's more life than death," he muttered. He looked at Linny. "And how are you doing, my dear?"

She walked over and gave him a big hug. "Better than you." But then she stopped, looked at him. "Or not." She looked back at Katie, who was busy muttering with her tape measure, then back at him again and grinned. "I am so happy."

He rolled his eyes. "Everybody needs to get out of my business," he muttered.

"No," Katie said. "They all share the same sentiment as I do."

"He's slow, but he finally got there," Linny declared. "I presume it was worth it."

At that, the two women chuckled, and Dave felt the heat spreading on his cheeks. "Enough of that," he said. "We have work to do."

"I'm running security and checking up on the others right now," Fallon stated from the side, as he put away his phone. "Bullard will be running security on Leia, and we have a bunch of stuff to set up. We've got a ship coming in with some prebuilds that we'll put together."

"What kind of a ship?" Dave asked.

"Not a fast one," Fallon stated, with a big smile, pointing out in the distance. Sure enough, there was a low slower-moving vessel, almost like a barge, coming toward them.

"So, now what? We're about to throw up a half-dozen huts or so?" Dave asked.

"That's part of it." Fallon nodded. "No reason not to, right?"

"No, none in the world." At that, Dave said, "You want to head back to the other boat to meet them, or are they coming in here?"

"I was just looking at the water. I think they can come in."

"That's one of the reasons this area is perfect," Dave stated. "It's deep right here."

CHAPTER 8

KATIE HEARD THE camaraderie between them, as the two men bounced ideas back and forth for building up a space for what they wanted here. She was only really concerned about food prep and a space to serve and eat, but they had to consider sleeping spaces as well.

Linny bounced all over the place, apparently just enjoying being here. "It's so beautiful."

"I know," Katie agreed. "I'm struggling with the whole wedding-in-paradise setup though."

"I just want to retire here," Linny stated, "even though retirement would be severely premature, but, man, this would be an amazing place to call home."

"I can't argue with you on that," Katie said. "It's really stunning. We've slept on the yacht the last couple nights, and that's been gorgeous too."

"I think I'm jealous," Linny said.

"Why?"

"Because I wanted to be here last night, and now that I've seen it, I just want to stay here for a couple weeks at least."

"I think that's what they've got in mind," Katie said, with a twist of her lips. "Like a retirement or a vacation center for everybody."

"What's not to like?" she replied. "And Bullard's very

good at taking care of people."

"That's what I was thinking." Katie smiled. "It would be nice to think that anybody in the company could use this." She looked around and couldn't help smiling. "I spend a lot of time on the yacht, depending on what Bullard's got going on, with traveling and offshore communication centers and such," she explained. "But, wow, I could cheerfully spend a week or two here every year."

"We might spend longer than that too," Fallon stated. "Depends on whether we end up setting up a center here or not."

"I think that would be ideal," Katie agreed.

"Well, now that we all think it's a great idea, we'll still have to convince Bullard of it," Dave said, with a smile.

Katie looked at him, laughed, and added, "Plus, we all have jobs to do, and his jobs keep the rest of us employed."

"There is that to consider as well," Fallon admitted, "but a compound on a South Pacific island? Hell yes!"

As Katie got back to sorting out her inventory of food supplies, she saw the vessel in the distance getting closer and closer. She watched in awe, when it finally got close enough, a small boat came off it and soared through the water at high speed toward the shore. Soon she saw Kano and Ryland. She smiled and lifted a hand, as they drifted past her. It was like having brought the army in because, with this team, they had enough men to start mobilizing equipment off the ship when it arrived.

Pretty quickly, they had a floating dock emplaced that she was just stunned about, and, as soon as the rest of the materials were unloaded, the captain would bring the yacht in and dock here. It sounded perfect to her that they would have a gangplank to get on and off the island, which would make moving the food and the setups a lot easier.

As it was, she wanted to stay on board and just watch as the men moved at the speed of lightning. She realized a bunch of other guys had arrived as well and had probably stayed on board. But it looked like all of Bullard's team was here now.

Bullard was still in the village with Leia, which made sense, depending on how the birth was going. Katie hoped everything was okay and that any complications were minor. That was the negative side of being here on the island because just no medical service was otherwise available. Even now, with Leia, Bullard, and Dave here, they all had tons of surgical experience but no equipment to speak of. They didn't have any testing equipment either and had only basic medical supplies. A lot of that could be taken care of perhaps, but was it worth it to provide medical supplies for a small village like that, with its lack of medical providers? She didn't know.

As Katie worked away, setting up dinner for everybody, and half expecting a head count much higher than originally planned, she turned and jumped, seeing Dave standing right behind her. "Oh my gosh," she said, patting her hand above her heart. "I didn't hear you."

"And here I was, trying to call you gently, so as not to scare you," he explained, with a smile.

"Oh, I don't think you succeeded." She laughed. "Come on with me back to the yacht and update me. So, where are we at?"

"We've got a ton unloaded, and we've got it organized. The entire crew is here, and several of their partners will be coming in later today," he noted. "So, there will be a few more trips back and forth to the mainland, and, by tomorrow, it looks like everybody will be here."

"I might need more food supplies then," she warned, getting into her boat and taking them back to the yacht.

He nodded. "Yeah, I wondered. That's one of the reasons I'm here, to check on what else you might need."

She did a rapid head count, as she thought about the number she would be feeding, and frowned. "Have we got barbecue grills yet?"

"Two large ones came off already," he replied, "and they'll be set up down on the extension of the beach deck."

She frowned at him. "Beach deck? Have you already got something like that set up? I so wanted to watch what all the guys were doing, but I needed to stay focused on my job here."

"It's a temporary setup for this visit," he said. "It will give us a good chance to test it out, as we work toward figuring out what we want for the future and getting that all in."

She smiled and nodded. "Well, I was just getting everything ready for dinner here," she said. "I wasn't exactly sure, with all the people coming and going, how many we are feeding tonight, but I've made sure there is a lot."

They reached the yacht, and she took him to her kitchen, to show him her progress so far.

He looked around, and his eyebrows shot up. "It doesn't look like that much," he noted cautiously.

She smiled. "Don't worry. The fridges are full. But I could certainly use more of that kind of equipment too."

"Yeah, I know. Refrigeration is an issue here," he said, "but we will be running fresh food daily from the mainland."

"That will help," she said cheerfully. "If I don't have to store that kind of thing, it will be a godsend."

"Exactly. Is there something I can help you with now?"

"All of this." She opened up a refrigerator to show him trays upon trays. "It all needs to go to the island, but we need a place for it first."

"Not a problem. I'll be back in a few minutes."

He went up on deck. Moments later, she heard the engine start up, and the yacht headed toward the new floating dock they had out. When she stepped outside, she stared, surprised. Actually maybe *stunned* was a better word, to see how much was now sitting at beach level and up at the area where Bullard's little shelter and bunk had been. There was also a massive stack of building materials off to the side. She imagined that the entire island would be thrumming with news over this. But it's kind of the way Bullard did things, … always in a big way, always with everything he needed. He didn't like to do without when it came to his people.

Just then Katie got a phone call from Ice.

"How's the island?" Ice asked her.

"It's gorgeous," she said. "Bullard and Leia are helping somebody deliver a baby right now. Plus, the old medicine woman took a bad blow to the head from one of the locals who was looking for medical attention—courtesy of Dave— but thankfully the medicine woman woke up and seems to be better." She then quickly explained everything that had gone on to date.

"Wow. So even in paradise he's finding plenty to keep him busy," Ice replied, but there was a note of anxiety in her voice. "Is it safe there?"

"I think so," Katie said. "I know the guys are certainly on full alert, just in case that gunman turns up again. It seems like he's been the source of all the trouble this trip."

"Right," she said.

"Are you coming?"

"Yes, we're leaving today. I'm actually calling from the airport," Ice stated. "We'll be in tomorrow."

"I'm so glad you're coming," Katie said warmly.

"Yeah, we're coming with the minister. We've got other plans we're kind of involved in too, so we'll see how this all works out." But a note of laughter was in her voice.

"Okay, I'll see you soon."

"Can't wait." And, with that, Ice hung up.

Katie turned to see Dave standing there, frowning.

"Was that Ice?"

"Yes." Not sure what she should tell him, she decided to not tell him anything. She immediately started taking trays out of the fridge. "Can you take these out?"

"Sure, but I wanted to show you how we've got it set up to make sure it's okay."

"You can show me as we carry these all out there." Katie grabbed two big trays herself.

Just then the captain joined them, but the confines in the galley were fairly small, so they passed the trays over, like a fire brigade, so everybody had two, and she grabbed two more.

"Okay, let's go," Katie said. "We'll have to come back for another round." They went up to the main deck, and then she walked down the new gangplank, so she could go from the yacht to the floating dock. She smiled. "Oh my gosh, this is exactly what we needed." Katie marveled at how fast the men had pulled it all together. "Is this like military equipment or something?"

"That's exactly what it is," Dave said, with a smile.

"It's perfect. And then what? Down the road you'll just

build something more permanent?"

"Correct." He chuckled.

As they got down a little farther, she could see that the flat decking area had been quadrupled in size. Some of it even went out over the water, obviously with some steel supports underneath—exposed as the tide shifted it.

"Is all that stable?" she asked in awe.

"Most definitely." Dave nodded. "Those over the water float."

She shook her head. "I've never seen anything go up so fast in my life."

"It's kind of what we do."

"Oh, I get that, but it never occurred to me that so few of you could do something like this so fast."

"Well, when it comes to mobilizing, accessibility is something we're specialists at." Dave walked down the ramp and called out, "Hey, Ry, have you got empty tables there for us?"

Ryland took one look and hopped up from what he was working on at the edge of the deck. "We will in just a second." And, just like that, they opened up four tables. Three trips later, Katie and her two helpers had everything she thought she needed for dinner. "What about Bullard? Where is he?"

"I haven't heard from him," Dave replied. "I should go see if I can get an idea of how far along they are with the birth."

"Did you ever find a path that leads directly through to the main area of the village?"

"Kano headed to the village right after we returned and located a decent-sized path, something we can all traverse." Dave turned and looked at Ryland. "Where is he?"

"He went to check on Bullard and Leia himself. He should be back soon." Ryland pulled out his phone, frowned. "I haven't heard anything from him."

They all looked at each other, and Katie felt her stomach knot.

"That could be a problem," Dave noted.

"Yeah." Ryland looked to Dave. "You coming with me?"

"Hell yes." Then he hesitated and turned to Katie.

"Oh, no, you don't." She raised one finger and shook her head. "Go. Lots of us are here."

He nodded, looked around at the rest of the team, all on alert. "We'll go check on Kano and Bullard and the progress with the baby. Everybody, keep your eyes and ears open, okay?"

"Keep in touch," Garret replied. Eton, Quinn, Cain, and Fallon all nodded, working nearby.

"Yeah, will do." With that, Dave took off with Ryland, as Katie stood here watching. Garret came over and looked at dinner. "Will this keep?"

"It will, for an hour or so. But we could always put it back on the yacht."

"Or not," Linny said, coming over. "I'm getting really hungry."

"Like, seriously hungry?" Katie asked. "Or like the food is now in front of you, so you're hungry?"

Linny laughed. "I can wait for Bullard to get back." She turned and looked in the direction Dave and Ryland went. "Maybe I can. Didn't they say it was a forty-five-minute walk?"

"Ryland got it down to about half an hour," Fallon noted, "but it's still a distance."

Linny nodded. "I hope we don't have to do that too often here, whether now or later as a vacation spot. Otherwise we might want to find a way to make it even faster, other than the skiff obviously. Especially when dealing with more people and transporting goods of any kind."

"What do you have in mind?"

"I don't know," she said, "but we should take a look at the area and see if there's a faster way to go on foot."

"I'll do that right now." Garret brought up an aerial view on his phone.

Linny smiled. "My laptop has a bigger screen. Let's go take a look."

Leaving them to deal with that, Katie walked around the deck, seeing several of the other men still finishing off bits and pieces. She marveled at the engineering that had brought this in so fast. She stood in front of a huge stack of what looked like prefab building walls and shook her head, realizing these were for the cabins that would go up almost as quickly.

Was it safe to leave the cabins behind after they left, she wondered, or would the islanders take them over, like squatters? Or would that be another issue? She didn't really know. She knew the locals marched to a different drummer here, so maybe it would be just fine. And Leia was well loved and even now was helping out the locals, so maybe that would keep all of this protected.

Smiling happily, Katie headed back to the kitchen on the yacht. What she really needed was to finish off the last few things, like the desserts, before everybody got back. Then they could all sit down at once and eat. And, if there was one thing that she really appreciated, it was food being served promptly.

She had gone to a lot of work to prepare all this, and it

was always nice when people were considerate and showed up on time. But somehow she figured that today, all bets were off.

DAVE FOLLOWED RYLAND as they headed past Leia's cabin to the pathway that showed years of use. But it wasn't very wide, and it was dark as they headed into the thicket of trees. "I wonder if this is a straight-through path."

"Yeah, I was wondering about clearing it out some, making it easier for walking," Ryland stated. "If this will be a path we take on a regular basis, we'll want something that's wider, more stable, and sure-footed."

"That we can actually see too, yet we don't really want to impact the environment either. So, if there's no reason to cut down trees, then I don't want to do it."

"Exactly. According to Bullard, it's about a thirty-minute walk, and it's—"

"I thought Leia said forty-five," Dave interrupted.

"A forty-five-minute stroll apparently," Ryland said, with a chuckle. "A thirty-minute walk if you're heading from point A to point B."

"Got it." And Dave did because a lot of people strolled in life, when they didn't have a certain place to be at a specific time. And walking with purpose could eat up the miles a whole lot faster.

They approached the midway point, as near as Ryland could tell. "Looks like a whole bunch of trails split off in here."

"I know the locals root around in here for nuts and berries and things too. I'm sure they have their favorite spots."

"Makes sense." Ryland nodded. "And if we knew which

one of these was the faster route, we could make better use of it."

"I still don't think we'll get it much faster," Dave said. "It's a pretty direct trail, considering."

As they carried on, they never saw another soul. "Is that weird?" Ryland asked. "You can walk for this long in this place and not actually come across another person."

"I like it though," Dave admitted.

"Oh, me too," Ryland agreed. "But it's amazing just how different this island life is. It must have been quite a culture shock for Leia coming from New York to this."

"And yet I think her soul probably craved it. She encountered so much destruction for her in New York."

"It's good that has all been taken care of now."

"They're clearing her name and reestablishing her medical credentials. She's apparently been getting requests to consider stepping back into the medical world. But I don't know that she's made a decision on what she wants to do."

"It can't be easy," Ryland murmured. "She probably lost a lot of faith in the system. And in people."

"True, but she still has a lot to offer."

"Maybe. A lot of doctors are out there in New York."

"No, listen," Dave said. "It's more than a maybe. Leia was one of the most talented surgeons they'd ever had. She was pioneering new techniques, which is what sparked so much jealousy."

"Have to love jealousy," Ryland mockingly said.

"Or not," Dave replied.

They walked for another ten minutes in silence, and up ahead they could see the path widening, with multiple paths joining in, as if this were a main walkway, which made sense.

As they came into the village, several of the people

stopped and stared. Dave smiled at them and lifted a hand and waved. "I've seen a lot of these people in the last couple days, but I'm not sure they're terribly comfortable with us being here."

"It all depends on how Leia's presence is taken."

"Well, I think it was decent. They greeted her warmly earlier."

"But you never really know with people."

"That's true enough." As they got closer, Dave looked up to see several of the younger women standing there, staring at them, then glancing back toward the hut where the old woman was. "Everybody is looking toward the one hut," he murmured to Ryland. "That's where the old woman lives."

"Do you think Bullard and Leia are in there, or are they helping the pregnant woman?"

"No idea, but what I'm really wondering is what happened to Kano."

They walked along through what was more of a central area, stopping in at the old medicine woman's place to check on her.

"She was outside last time I saw her," Dave noted.

"There's not much difference here between outside and inside, is there? And the fresh air is probably a big help."

"Maybe. Where are Bullard and Leia though?"

"I don't know." Ryland looked around.

Dave recognized one of the men he'd spoken to last time. He walked over and motioned at the medicine woman's hut. "How is she?"

He just shrugged and looked at him and stared a little more suspiciously at Ryland.

"And what about Leia? Where is Leia?" Dave asked.

The local looked at Dave in surprise and then shrugged.

"It's almost as if he doesn't know where Leia is, and I don't like that at all."

"And we're up against the damn language barrier too."

"Broken English, for those who do the trips to the mainland," he said. "The old woman has a decent command of English though."

"Well, let's go in and see if she's awake. With that, they headed toward her hut and stepped inside, finding it empty. "So, where is she?" Ryland asked.

"Unless she's been moved to somebody who can look after her, I don't know." Dave pulled out his phone and quickly sent Bullard a message, asking where he was. When Dave didn't get an answer, he sent a message, confirming that he and Ryland were in the village, to Garret and Fallon, but hadn't found Bullard yet, explaining how the old lady was missing from her hut. Immediately his phone rang.

"Are you saying this is a problem?" Fallon asked.

"I'm saying, I don't know. I'd feel better if we could find them or get ahold of them."

"You and me both. I thought somebody already headed over here. Didn't Kano go looking for them?"

"Yeah, that's why Ryland and I headed this way because we couldn't get a response from him either." Just then Dave caught sight of one of the women who had been standing beside the old lady before. She stared at him, her eyes huge, as if she wanted to tell him something.

Dave whispered into the phone, "Hold on. I'm hoping to get some information." Instead of hanging up the call, he walked over to her, crouched down because she was low to the ground beside a tree, and he asked quietly, "What's going on?"

She glanced around nervously, then pointed to a hut off to the side.

"Is that where Leia is?"

She nodded slowly.

"Is she alone?"

She shook her head.

"Is Bullard with her?"

She shrugged at that.

Maybe she didn't know who Bullard was. Then he remembered the one guy. "Is Pietro there?"

She nodded immediately, her movement emphatic, and the fear had returned to her gaze.

"Can they leave?"

She shook her head.

"Okay." And then Dave stopped to look at the old medicine woman's empty hut. "Where is your medicine woman?"

Her face turned sad.

He nodded. "Okay. I'll be back here in a few minutes." He walked over to where Ryland waited for him. "I don't know how good the intel is," he admitted, "but it looks like Bullard and Leia are being held by Pietro in that hut over there." He motioned quietly to the hut in the distance. "I would suspect that even now we're being watched."

"And do you think they saw whoever gave us that information? Is she in danger?"

"I think at this point they'd have to quarantine the entire community," Dave said, "because most villagers won't help Pietro if he's hurting them. My impression from our informant is that the old medicine women is dead. I fear that Pietro took her out for good this time."

Ryland looked at him in surprise. "That's not good."

"It's not good for a lot of reasons," Dave agreed. "She seemed to have control of much of the population."

"Except for this guy you've been having trouble with, right?" Ryland turned casually to look around. "So, we're gonna need to disappear and come at this from another angle."

"I'd say so. If Bullard's in there and being held, he knows we'll be coming for him and he'll be watching for us."

"But, if they hurt Leia or if they need Leia for something, that's a different story."

"I shot Pietro right in the wrist on his gun hand that first night we had trouble, so he may have Leia working on that. I'm betting the pregnant woman isn't inside anymore," he muttered. As he turned to ask the other young woman, Dave found her gone.

"We also have to consider that it all may be a trap," Ryland said.

"I know. Nothing here is clear-cut."

"Not exactly how we thought we would be spending our time here."

"We always knew that somebody here had exposed her location," Dave noted. "But we'd assumed that everything related to New York was over with, since we dealt with Bullard's half brother and that murdering surgeon back there."

"And doesn't that just beat all," Ryland said, with a headshake. "We were all looking for a bit of a break and some downtime to celebrate the end of the trouble we've been fighting these past months. It'll really piss me off if this local problem takes away from the joy and peace and quiet that we came here for."

"Not to mention all the weddings."

Ryland smiled. "I don't know that there will be more than one, but we're sure as hell hoping for that one for Bullard's sake."

"Right." Dave didn't have any more to say on that point, his mind carefully processing all the information he had. Then he spoke quietly, "I suggest we walk through the village, as if we're leaving, then circle back around."

"Do we suspect that these guys have any warfare experience? Or intelligence? Are we looking at somebody who's likely to set a trap for us?"

"We can't discount human slyness," Dave admitted. "But do they have any actual experience? Other than the silencer on his gun and the wetsuit, I have no clue. But it would be wrong of us to assume that taking them down will be a simple job."

"I guess the question is, do we need backup?"

"Seeing how backup is at least thirty minutes away, I suggest we call for it now. But we need to do as much recon as we can."

With that, Ryland was already on the phone, letting the rest of the guys know what was going on.

Dave watched the area as they walked past, both of them acting as unconcerned and as casual as they could. As they got to the other end of the village, they stepped into the trees, off the path. Then, moving carefully and watching behind them, they circled back around to the hut they had been told Leia was in. They hadn't gotten very far, when Dave pointed to a sentry standing off to the side. "So, one guard is there for sure."

"Interesting," Ryland whispered. "Not exactly what I was expecting."

"No, but, hey, the fact that they've even got somebody

posted means they're aware that they could be coming under attack."

"Obviously." Ryland nodded. "We've got troops coming in here any minute, so let's set up our own positions. Then we'll wait."

"Good enough." Dave glanced at Ryland as they settled down for what would likely be a twenty-minute wait. "So, are you really hoping to get married here?"

"I am," he said, with a grin. "Tabi's been kind of slow about it though."

"She doesn't want to commit or what?" Dave asked.

"No, she's committed but doesn't want to get married *now*, which seems to be a common theme at the moment."

"Well, maybe after she sees Bullard and Leia getting married, she'll change her attitude."

"Maybe." Ryland shrugged. "I suggested a multiple wedding, but she said no, that Bullard had to have his day. I'm not at all sure that Bullard cares though."

"Nope, I don't think he cares one bit," Dave agreed. "He just wants to get married and call this a done deal, so he doesn't have to worry about it anymore."

"I wonder what Ice thinks of this," Ryland asked.

"She's happy for him. Ice is linked to Bullard no matter what and knows about most happenings anyway," he noted. "The pair of them are pretty much in touch with everything going on in the world."

"Well, that's true with Terk as well," Ryland said.

"And that's a bizarre relationship. I've known him for a long time, and, if Terk says move, you move," he murmured. Just then Dave's phone rang, and he looked down at the ID. *Private Number.* Dave answered with a question. "Who is this?"

"You were just talking about me," Terk said. "However, you've got trouble on the island."

"Yeah, we're just figuring that out," he stated. "You could have told us about fifty minutes earlier."

"Wouldn't have changed anything," he said. "You're surrounding one hut, but I think it's all happening at another place."

"What do you mean by *another place*?"

"I think—I think it's too simplistic to believe it's all right there. I think another hut is involved."

"Okay," he said. "Any idea where?"

"If you head to the left, I'd say maybe"—and he stopped—"fifty yards, you'll find another hut. It looks old, abandoned. It's a prisoner shed."

"Okay," Dave said, "I'll take a look."

"This one isn't a big thing," Terk stated, "but don't mess it up. Let's not have all these weddings wind up as funerals instead."

"What do you know about all the weddings?" he asked.

He chuckled. "Let's just say, it will be an island of celebration pretty soon."

After Terk hung up, Dave shook his head, looking at Ryland. "You won't believe it, but that was Terk."

"Speak of the devil." Ryland stared at Dave with a smirk. "How the hell does he do that all the time?"

"I don't know, but he does, and he's just so damn good at it that I find it a little freaky. He also said that all the action isn't in the hut we're watching but another one somewhere in the back here."

And, with that, they stepped a little farther away, came up behind the sentry, and dropped him easily. Propping the guy up on the ground against a tree, Dave left him in place, in case anybody was taking a look; it appeared he was sitting here, his arm resting on his knee. Then they headed off to the side.

Up ahead, Dave saw something hidden in the trees and underbrush. He pointed. "That's it right there."

Ryland looked at it, frowned. "Dammit, Terk is right again."

"He almost always is," Dave said. "We just don't work with him that often."

"Levi should get Terk to join his team, what with his brother Merk there already."

"I don't think Terk does very well working for people," Dave said quietly. "He's fairly tormented by everything in his world."

"Can you imagine not having any peace and quiet from this stuff in your head all the time?" Ryland frowned.

"I know. I think that's part of the problem. He doesn't ever get to shut this off."

"Let's go take a look at what we've got here." Ryland nodded toward the hidden hut. At that, he went a step forward.

Dave touched his arm and whispered, "I think we have more sentries."

They dropped to the ground and watched two men heading in their direction.

CHAPTER 9

KATIE WAS BUSY back at Leia's cabin, trying to make the best use of this little space. She was turning this cabin into a prep kitchen, where they could store food off the yacht, using it more for washing and cleaning up. As Fallon and Linny walked closer, Katie looked up, smiled, and heard the two of them talking, as they walked past the cabin, not really seeing her.

"I'm not sure I want to get married right now," Linny said.

"We don't have to," Fallon stated. "But there's definitely something magical in the air here."

"I don't want to be caught up in the magic," she replied in a dry tone.

"You know by now that I love you, and absolutely nothing will change that, right?"

"I know," she said, smiling at him. "Let me think about it."

"You do that." He grinned broadly. "I've asked, and you've said yes. It's just a matter of setting the time."

She laughed at that. "That's very true."

Katie smiled, wondering if she needed to triple the quantity of champagne, just so all the team and their partners could gather here and celebrate this time together—and not just at the wedding but beyond. A lot of them were here, and they may extend their stays. Maybe this island vacation was just what needed to happen. For all of them.

And something *was* quite magical about this place.

Once in a while, she carried coffee and cold punch, made from a variety of juices, around to all, going from couple to couple. Katie found that the women were all busily working with the men. Some were helping to erect the prefab walls, building cabins before their eyes. Some were cleaning out ground cover to allow for a new cabin. Some stood off to the side, out of the way, taking photos and videos to remember this time.

Katie stood by, smiling, looking around at all the people here to celebrate Bullard and Leia's wedding.

When she brought out a big bowl of punch, everybody oohed and aahed, and the women came racing to help. Katie laughed and waved them away. "I'm just working away, doing my thing."

"That's the thing," Izzie said. "You're working, and the men are working and, while we're helping where we can, we are almost on a holiday. It feels strange that way."

"You can help me if you want, but I know the men need to get cabins and whatever built and get it up fast—before tonight, I guess." As Katie turned to look, she shook her head because already two cabins were up. "Wow."

"I know," Izzie said. "It's like they're pros at this."

"Are they really trying to get eight cabins up by tonight?" Linny asked.

Katie nodded. "We all need a place to crash, starting tonight."

And then Linny quickly rolled off the names of the team. "Not Bullard. I suppose he and Leia will at least take over the yacht for their wedding night. But we have"—and she raised a finger for each name mentioned—"Ry, Cain, Eton, Garret, Kano, Fallon, Quinn, and Dave. Yeah, eight of the remaining team members."

"I think they're also hoping to get some kind of cover up for the ceremony itself, in case the weather changes." Katie pointed out to the ocean. It was still blue skies and white clouds, but the storms here came up quickly.

Izzie nodded. "I guess if that changes, it could be quite different here."

"Maybe. As long as it's still warm, it won't matter." And, with that, Katie headed back to the yacht, as she worked away on her supply list. It would be something she had to stay on top of. Already she didn't have enough cutlery for the wedding. And that lack would irritate her. She didn't want plastic out here at all, but she was multitasking with her kitchen tools as it was. She had hot soapy water in the sink all the time.

Still, she kept herself busy, as she prepped a menu list for the next three days. Then she looked at her current inventory of food and what more she needed. She added 50 percent more in alcohol, another 50 percent in extra hors d'oeuvres. If the team pulled off their joint weddings plan—which seemed nebulous at best and no one was updating her on this—Katie had to accommodate that big surprise too. She wasn't sure that would happen, but, given the moonlight, the magic, and the romance in the air, she wouldn't be at all surprised.

At the same time, she wondered if she should be worrying about the opposite effect, what with the danger they'd all been through. But then she had no reason to think that anything untoward would happen anyway, not with the whole team here. So far, everybody had been delighted to be on the island, even though they were hard at work putting things together. And, as long as Bullard and Leia were fine, then it was hard to imagine anything else could go wrong.

Just as she thought that, the captain came down below to the galley, carrying a handgun. She looked at it, up at him, and raised an eyebrow. "Trouble?"

He nodded grimly. "Leia and Bullard are missing."

She sucked back her breath. "Jesus. Do the others know?"

"They've been called to help Ryland and Dave in the village. I'm headed over to the island to keep an eye on the women." He hesitated. "I don't really want to leave you here alone."

"I'm fine. Just leave me my handgun," she said, waving her hand around the kitchen. "I'll be right here, so that won't be an issue."

He frowned, thought about it, and then agreed. "Okay. I'll keep the rest of them in one spot down there."

"You do that, but don't forget to let me know when it's over, so I can stop worrying and relax."

He smiled. "I'll come and update you. But first I'll get you a gun and bring it to you."

"Good enough." She immediately started baking because, whenever she was upset or happy, baking was one of the things she turned to. If nothing else, she could at least hope for a quick end to this. Otherwise she'd have everybody on the island gaining weight from her pastries and other goodies. That wouldn't be a bad thing. It had been a very difficult few months for this group, and nearly all the men had been injured, one way or another. A few extra pounds would probably be a good thing, a healing thing.

Sam popped in just long enough to lay her gun on the

opposite counter. She nodded her thanks. Katie sighed, then got back to work.

She had favorite requests marked down for each and every one of the guys because she had cooked for all of them at various times, but she didn't know a whole lot about the women's preferences. Katie frowned, wondering if that would be an issue, and then decided to just go ahead and do what she always did, offering an assortment.

She immediately made some afternoon tea scones, as if later today there would be a bloody party after rescuing Bullard and Leia. Katie shook her head, knowing it was foolish, but it kept her mind occupied and her hands busy. And that was just as important to her.

The last thing she wanted to do was worry about someone coming after anybody on this island. She thought for sure the danger would have passed, but they had witnessed enough trouble by now that she knew it was too much to hope for. A lot of the team remained around here now, hopefully enough that she didn't have to worry about anybody attacking them. At least that was the hope. Not a whole lot else she could do but keep busy, so that's what she did.

Tea scones done. And then she started in on pies. She could always freeze them and pull them out in a couple days. She didn't have a very big freezer here, but she did have one. She made fresh strawberry pie because some of the strawberries weren't looking as good as they should. Then she made a spinach and cheese quiche pie, all the while trying to push out the negative thoughts and keep her mind occupied on happier things.

When her phone rang, it was Dave. She quickly answered it. "Oh my God, are you okay?"

"I'm okay," he said hoarsely. "Are you okay?"

"I'm fine." She eased back against the counter, a hand to her chest. "I thought for sure all this was over with."

"It is now. Bullard and Leia have been found. They're fine. The guy who I shot was holding them, trying to get Leia to fix his wrist. Ryland and I had tracked them to where they were being held and were waiting for backup, when Kano broke it all up. Remember? He'd gone to check on them, and then we didn't hear any more? That's because he'd caught on and could get right in there with them and hide, until he got a chance to make a move."

"Of course, and was Leia able to fix his hand?"

"She got the bleeding stopped, but he needs surgery to fix all the bone damage. She also gave him a hard talking to. The medicine woman is dead. She didn't survive his second attack, after another argument with him. So now the rest of the tribe is very angry with Pietro, and they're kicking him out. He's banished and has to leave the island today."

"Hasn't he left already?"

"Not yet," Dave said. "Well, at least they hope he has, but he slipped away from them."

"That's not good. He's one of those guys you never can trust."

"That's one of the reasons I'm calling," he said. "I just want to make sure you're okay."

"Why wouldn't I be?" she asked cautiously.

"No reason."

His rush to reassure her was not working. "Okay, that's not making me feel any better," she muttered.

"I'm on the way back. Does that make you feel better?"

"If you were here on the yacht already with me, it would, yes. But I'm used to being alone, so it's fine."

"Ten minutes," he said.

"Good enough." And Katie paused, frowned. "Of course I run all my plans through Bullard, but does Leia know about all this wedding planning he and I've done here?"

"Yes," he confirmed.

"Glad to hear that."

"Have we got enough supplies?"

"I think so." Katie laughed. "I just wanted to make sure that Leia herself is part of all this."

"She just wanted a simple island wedding," he replied. "Oh, and all the villagers have been invited."

"*Ohhh*," she said, with a slow exhale of breath.

"Is that a problem?" he asked curiously.

"Only in terms of food." She sighed. "Okay, so that's what I'll do next—try to figure out what else I might need."

"I think they'll be bringing some island fare too."

"That's good. That'll help," she replied, "because we still don't have ourselves set up here. Any chance we can push the wedding back a few days?" she asked hopefully.

"I don't think Bullard would be up for that. He wants to make sure they're married as soon as possible."

She laughed at that. "You mean, now that he's waited this long ..."

"Exactly."

She smiled. "Okay, you'd better get your ass back here in ten minutes."

"Will do."

She hung up, and, as she turned around, she cried out. "Oh my God! What are you doing here?" Right there in front of her was a man with a heavily bandaged wrist. And a gun.

"You'll take this boat back to the mainland," he ordered,

"and we'll sell it, so I have some way to make a living from here on out."

"Do you really think, with all the men on shore, that you'll get away like this?"

"If you drive us away from here, they'll just think you're going for supplies."

He really didn't understand how things worked because she'd never actually piloted this yacht, beyond messing around out in the open ocean in calm seas. She'd certainly done plenty of that, but she had never pulled into a port and docked it or anything. Besides, it was still tied onto the floating dock out there.

"You don't understand," she replied gently. "This can't happen. If you want to get away—like you're supposed to get away—you need to just leave."

"How am I supposed to do that? Nobody would give us a lift."

"I think you've used up all the goodwill anybody here has for you after killing the medicine woman, who I understand is a blood relative to you."

"Stop talking and drive this boat," he yelled.

Katie huffed. "I can't even start the engine. The captain has the keys."

He glared at her in frustration and looked around, as if trying to find an answer. "You must have money."

"Money?" she repeated "Why the hell would I have money out here?"

"I have to leave." He waved the gun around, with a panicked look.

"I get that, but what is it you expect from me?"

Just then a man's voice came from behind Pietro. "It doesn't matter what he expects because he's not getting it."

She looked up to see Dave glaring at Pietro. The guy turned the handgun, lifting it to point it at Dave. But Dave grabbed his injured wrist and squeezed, then turned his right fist into a battering ram and hit the guy as hard as he could on the jaw.

He went down in a heap.

She frowned in disgust and glared at Pietro. "I don't know if anybody is planning a trip to the mainland, but he needs an escort. That's what he was trying to do, just get out of here and get to the mainland, before the rest of the island found out he hadn't left yet. We should help him do that. Hand him off to the police there."

"In that case, we'll arrange for somebody to take him." And, with that, Dave yanked Pietro up, tossed him over his shoulder in a fireman's carry, and headed to the main part of the dock.

AS DAVE UNCEREMONIOUSLY dumped the unconscious man's body at the bottom of the ramp, Bullard came over and stared at Pietro, then looked at Dave. "Is Katie okay?" His voice was harsh.

"She's fine. I might not be, but she is."

"No, I understand that completely," Bullard snapped.

"So, Pietro needs a lift to the mainland. And now."

"Get somebody from the island to take him," Leia suggested. "They should look after their own."

"Can we trust them to get rid of him?"

"He's been banished. They should have taken him before, but he disappeared."

"Looks like he came here, hoping to steal the yacht," Bullard added. "Somebody needs to contact the villagers."

It took less than an hour, but they had somebody from the village come around via boat on the same side of the waterway that Dave had traveled many times. Soon Pietro was loaded into the boat, now conscious and tied up, but sullen as all hell. In no time the boat was underway, hopefully headed for the authorities on the mainland.

"Do you think that's the last we've seen of him?" Katie asked.

"The islanders won't take him back," Leia said quietly. "That's his punishment for the death of the old medicine woman."

"Not to mention all the other crimes he's been involved in," Bullard added. "He had way more than that coming."

"I know." She patted his arm, then hugged him tight.

Even as Dave watched, Leia linked fingers with Bullard. "And now we let it go. We came here for a holiday."

"And to get married," he said, squeezing her fingers.

She smiled, reached out, and kissed his cheek. "Tomorrow."

"We can do it today," he suggested.

She laughed. "The wedding will be tomorrow. You'll be fine."

"Says you."

Dave had to chuckle. "You're really in a rush, huh?"

"I feel like a new man," Bullard admitted, "completely different."

"Good, so tomorrow's the big ceremony."

At that, Leia turned and shook her head. "No. Not a big ceremony. It will be short and simple."

"Okay," he said. "If you say so."

"I do," she replied. "I'm not all about pomp and ceremony. I'm not about anything other than a simple vow between the two of us." And, with that, she turned and walked toward her place.

Dave looked at Bullard. "You still happy?"

"Insanely happy," he said, with a big smile. "And you?"

"Very. It's not what I expected either."

"Maybe not, but I'm very happy for you. Unless you'll leave Africa, that is."

"Nope. I'm hoping to convince her to come live with me. But I'm trying not to push it."

He laughed at that. "Right. Seems like we're walking a delicate balance here."

"And that's okay too," Dave said. "This has happened really quickly."

"No, it hasn't," Bullard argued. "It's been painfully slow, if you ask me. You've been a long time getting up to snuff."

"Hey! You're not the first person to tell me that though," he admitted.

"Pretty soon you'll be like I am, in a rush to make it official—to ensure she can't change her mind."

Dave smiled. "Is that what it is?"

"No, I don't think so," he replied. "I just want to know that it's over and done with."

"If you say so." Dave smirked.

Bullard shook his head. "That's not it either. I just want to begin my new life, with her, all properly wed in front of all of you."

"I agree with that." Dave turned toward the yacht. "Maybe I'll head back out and check up on Katie."

"You do that. We'll work on the rest of these huts for the moment, but I really want to start looking at building plans soon."

"What are you thinking about?"

"We've acquired quite a bit of property here, or we will have very soon," he added. "I think we should build a small eco-friendly compound, hiring lots of the locals for the construction, as well as for maintenance and such, with everything digitally set up, so anyone can come at any time."

"Yeah, I figured that would be next. We'll need to take some measurements, get some topographical data, all while we're here, so we can draw up the plans when we get back."

"Yeah, we can do that—after tomorrow," he said. "Getting married is really all I can think about." And, with a big grin, he turned and headed up after Leia.

CHAPTER 10

THE NEXT MORNING dawned bright and clear. The wedding ceremony was set for nine in the morning, and Katie had been up for hours. By the time Dave got back on board again, he looked almost as rattled as she felt. He held out his arms; she walked into them and crashed.

"My God," she said. "It's always such fun, but it's so much work."

"But we're almost there."

"Damn good thing." She laughed.

He looked at her and asked, "Anything else I can take down?"

She pointed to the stacks of food and dishes sitting on the side. "All of that needs to go."

He nodded and headed down the dock with his arms full. After that, it went quickly, as everybody came to help. By the time it was all set up, Dave came back, held out his hand, and asked, "Are you ready? The ceremony will start soon."

She nodded, her mind still on all the things that had to be done for the meals later in the day.

"It's okay. Everything is set up."

"Is it though?" she asked anxiously. "I know this is really important to Bullard."

"What's important to Bullard is the part that will happen in a few minutes," Dave said. "The rest of it is not on his mind at all. I guarantee it."

She looked up at him, smiled. "I get that, but at the same time—"

"Nope," he said, "believe me. This is not Bullard's worry. He probably can't eat, before or after. Not that he doesn't recognize all you've done here."

And then she grabbed Dave's hand, and together they walked around to make sure the reception area was ready. She had managed to weave the offerings from the islanders into her tables laden with her brunch menu, and it couldn't have been more perfect. Then they headed up to where Leia's small cabin sat, where everybody waited.

Leia was inside, still hidden from view.

Katie and Dave followed the path to the edge of the water, where the actual ceremony would take place. Katie smiled happily. "It really is very stunning."

"It is, indeed," Dave agreed. "Now we'll just step over here." As they watched and waited, music started, an island melody. She realized that the islanders had come down with drums and were starting the ceremony themselves.

Katie laughed with joy as Bullard appeared, not in a tuxedo or in a suit, but in shorts and a Hawaiian shirt, a huge grin on his face. Standing beside him wasn't Dave or any of the guys from his team. It was Levi. She looked up in surprise at Dave.

"Levi is his best man," Dave whispered gently.

"I've been so involved with the food that I never considered who was in the wedding party."

And there, off to the side stood Ice, holding their toddler, who Katie hadn't really heard any details about, and had yet to meet. As they waited, Leia slowly made the trip down the makeshift aisle in a simple sundress, colorful wildflowers in her hand, one of the elders from the island at her side.

Katie gasped in joy. "Look at that."

"Nice and simple." Dave nodded.

Leia wore one of her long flowing dresses, in a shimmery fabric, almost with a gold silken look. And then she stepped up next to Bullard, joining the minister who stood behind them up on the rocks and did the service. The sun played upon the ocean, as the water sparkled beside them, and a gentle breeze lifted the leaves around them, letting the women's hair float softly, as spoken words and promises were made forever.

Katie squeezed Dave's fingers. "It's magical," she whispered.

And, when the final pronouncement was made, Leia threw her arms around Bullard's neck and hugged him close. He lowered his head and kissed her for all to see. The crowd burst into laughter and cheers, and finally the two stepped back, holding each other close.

Bullard said, "And that, my friends, is how it's done."

Ice chuckled. "Well, it is for some of us." She walked over, kissed Bullard gently on the cheek, and hugged Leia. "Welcome to the family."

Tears immediately sprang to Leia's face. "Thank you. I'm not sure I've ever heard anything nicer."

"Bullard has been part of our family for a very long time," Ice stated, "and we are so happy he found you."

Just then Ryland stepped up to the newlyweds. "So"— and he looked at Bullard—"if you don't mind."

Bullard, with a big grin, swept Leia into his arms and moved her back a little bit, as Ice and Levi stood off to the side.

Ryland walked up to Tabi and held out his hand. "I asked you a question earlier."

She nodded slyly. "You asked me to marry you, and I said yes."

"True," he said. "Then I asked you to marry me today."

"And the answer is ... yes," she said, with a great big smile.

Together they walked up to the minister, and right there, in front of everybody, were married as well. There were gasps of joy as another simple ceremony happened, and tears flowed in copious amounts as everybody realized just how special this was.

And dammit if Kano and his partner, Catherine, didn't step up right afterward.

Katie watched openmouthed, as one by one, every one of Bullard's men and their partners, silently but happily, stepped up and got married, all on the same day.

"I thought they were just talking about this. Was this all preplanned?" Katie asked Dave.

"Well, it was kind of free-flowing and preplanned, in the sense that the women hadn't given a definitive yes. But, once they got to the island and realized what it would be like to get married here, I think the guys worked on it pretty hard to convince their partners."

By the time Quinn stepped up to the preacher with Izzie, the place was cheering madly, and the two were married just as fast. Then Quinn turned to look at Dave, raised an eyebrow. "Your turn."

Dave shook his head and smiled. "No, not today."

Katie frowned. "Why not?"

He looked at her in surprise. "I didn't want to rush

you."

She smiled. "You know what? You're right. You shouldn't have rushed me. I think I'll rush you instead." And she linked her fingers with his and dragged him up to the altar.

He protested the whole way, but everybody was clapping, cheering them on. When they stood in front of the minister, Katie turned to look at Dave. "I've waited years to truly have you in my life, but, if you're not ready, then, no. We won't do this right now."

He stopped and stared at Katie, feeling the tears burning the back of his throat. "I've waited a long time too," he murmured. "I just didn't think this would ever happen again."

She kissed him ever-so-gently. "It's time for *us* now. It's time for all of us," she said, with a hand motion to include the others. "It's time to let the ghosts of the past rest in peace, while we make new lives, new futures, for all of us."

Dave linked his fingers with hers and turned to the minister. "Say what you need to say, but the bottom line is, I do!" Everybody loudly cheered, and Dave believed his heart was breaking, as it was so full of joy. He'd never thought he would come to this point again. But, as he quickly shared vows with Katie at his side, he realized that nothing had felt so right in a very long time. Afterward he kissed her before all his good friends and held her close.

All the newly proclaimed couples swayed gently in the arms of their spouses, as the river rose and fell around them, spurred on by the morning tides of the ocean, while the sun shone brightly, and the breeze gently moved around them.

Finally Katie turned, looked around at everybody, and said, "This was unexpected, but I have to tell you that it is pretty damn perfect. But, more than that, brunch is ready!"

"You should see what she's got. It's amazing!" Dave added.

"I went all-out," she explained, "because it was Bullard's wedding. I had no clue it would be my wedding breakfast too."

With tears and laughter, she led Dave and the rest of the crowd to the deck area, where the tables were laden with a beautiful brunch buffet. Another table held champagne, fresh coffee, and a stunningly beautiful punch fountain. It was a tropical breakfast for the wedding party and guests and for everyone from the island. Nothing had ever looked better.

Dave stood here and stared at the complete chaos that she had turned into something so extraordinary, and he turned, snatched her up, and held her close. "Did I tell you how perfect you are?" he asked.

"Nope." She patted his cheek. "The good thing is, now I know you'll have lots of time to remind me."

He burst out laughing. "Well, there is some truth to that." He paused. "We didn't even talk about—" And he stopped, shaking his head.

"Like, where will we live? Where will we work? How will we sort it all out and all those good things?"

"Yeah," he said, with a crooked smile.

"That's because none of it is as important as our relationship," she replied. "We'll work it out."

"Are you still okay to work for Bullard?"

"She damn well better be," Bullard roared from beside them. "I'm not having you guys all split off and leave me now."

Katie looked at him and grinned. "No, I'll still be the

same old Katie," she said.

He grinned, grabbed her into a great big hug, and then literally picked her up and handed her over to Dave. His other arm was snaked around Leia, tucking her in close.

Katie was still laughing, as Dave placed her down on the ground gently. "See? It's really not a problem," she explained. "I don't know how big your room is at the compound, but maybe it'll be big enough for me too."

He immediately kissed her and held her close. "I actually have a suite to myself," he stated, "so, technically, yes. There is plenty of room for you."

"And, if you want to start a family down the road," she murmured, gently touching her lips to his, "we might have to look at getting another house."

At that, Bullard snorted. "Hell no. There is plenty of land at that compound, so I suggest we start building houses. If we all have kids sometime in the future, then we'll need playgrounds and spaces for them to run around and play, and maybe a small soccer field or baseball field," he said, warming up with enthusiasm.

Leia laughed. "So far, Levi and Ice are the only ones with children," she said, "so there is definitely time to plan for more little ones."

Bullard looked at Ice, who was grinning madly. Her beautiful blond son beamed in her arms. "What do you know that you haven't shared?"

Ice immediately dropped a hand to her rounded belly. "Number two is on the way," she proudly said, "You guys need to catch up."

At that, cheers erupted once again, as Levi wrapped her up in his arms, his one-year-old son tucked up against his shoulder. "Dammit, Bullard, now you finally made a change that you won't regret."

"I know," Bullard said. "It feels so damn good to be at this stage of our lives."

"It only gets better," Levi added. "I promise. It'll only get better."

Dave looked down at Katie and whispered, "What do you think about that pronouncement?"

"I think it's perfect," she said, her voice gentle, "because, when you think about it, look at all we've been through. Look at all of the things in our lives, the ups and downs, the people we've met, the people we've fallen in love with, and those we've lost—one way or another."

He leaned over and kissed her gently.

"This is the cycle of life. We fall down, and we stand back up again, and we start all over, if we need to. At this moment in time, we're all exactly where we want to be," she said. "Look at us. This is the beginning of a whole new future, and I, for one, can't wait."

EPILOGUE

ICE LANDED BACK home in the States again, tired, worn out, and wearing a big smile on her face. She couldn't wait to get inside and relax. The island holiday had been absolutely stupendous, along with all the marriages and seeing everybody so happy, so joyful. It had been amazing, especially since they had all been through so much. A happy surprise was that Ice felt a bond with Leia that she hadn't expected but was delighted to have.

As she walked through the kitchen a couple hours later, feeling like she was back home and getting into the swing of things, their team was gathered around the huge dining room table, and Levi was filling them in on as many details as he could. She poured herself a coffee, sat down with them, and, when her phone rang, she smiled. "Hey, Terk. How're you doing?" She put the call on Speakerphone.

"I'm okay." But his voice was distracted and tight.

"Terk?" Merk called from across the dining room table. He got up and walked closer to the phone and sat across from Levi. "You don't sound too good, bro."

"I'm fine. Or I will be. Right now, things are blown to shit."

"As in literally?" Merk asked.

"The entire group," Terk said. "They're all gone. I had six team members. and they're all gone."

"Dead?"

"No." Terk took a deep breath. "I'm not making sense. I'm sorry."

"Take it easy," Ice said, her voice calm and reassuring. "What do you mean, they're all gone?"

"All their abilities are gone," he stated. "Something's happened to them. Somebody has deliberately done something to each and every one of them to remove whatever special senses they utilized—what we have been utilizing for the last ten years for the government." His tone was bitter. "When they closed us down, they promised that the team would never rise again, but I didn't expect them to attack us personally."

"What are you talking about?" Merk asked in alarm.

"I don't know yet," Terk replied., "I'm going under to find out exactly what the hell's going on."

"What can we do to help?" Levi asked.

Terk gave a broken laugh. "That's not why I'm calling. Well, it is, but it isn't."

Ice looked at Merk, who frowned as he stared at the phone, listening to his brother's voice, and the completely confusing words coming out of his mouth.

"Terk, you're not making sense again," Merk stated.

Terk took a long slow deep breath. "Tell Stone to open the gate," Terk said. "She's out there."

"Who's out there?" Everybody in the dining room stared at the phone. Levi hopped up, looked outside, and shrugged.

"She's coming up the road now. You have to let her in."

"Why?"

"Because she's been harnessed with C-4."

"Jesus," Levi said. "Is it live?"

"It is, and she's been sent to you."

"Well, that's an interesting move," Ice noted, her voice sharp. "Who's after her?"

"I'm thinking it's rebels within the Iranian government."

"And why her?"

"I don't know," Terk said in complete frustration. "I also don't know how they got her so close to you. Or how they pinned your connection to me," he added. "I've been very careful."

"We can look after ourselves," Ice said immediately. "But who is this woman to you?"

"She's pregnant," he explained, "so that adds to the intensity here."

"Understood. So where is the father?"

There was silence on the other end.

Merk spoke up again. "Terk, talk to us."

"She's carrying my baby, Merk," Terk said, his voice heavy.

Merk, his expression turning grim, stared at Ice. "How do you know her, Terk?"

"Brother, you don't understand," Terk said. "I've never met this woman before in my life." And, with that, the phone went dead.

This concludes Book 9 of Bullard's Battle: Bullard's Best.
Read about Damon's Deal: Terkel's Team, Book 1

Damon's Deal: Terkel's Team (Book #1)

Welcome to a brand-new series from *USA Today* best-selling author Dale Mayer, where dark-ops SEALs have special senses and skills, needed to solve intrigue, betrayal, and ... murder. A series with all the elements you've come to love, plus so much more, ... including psychics!

With the bulk of his team down, Terk tries to establish a new base, while struggling to heal the team through the special connection each has. Damon is concerned about finding Tasha, one of their admins, and keeping her safe. But, without any secure place to take her, Damon's making do with the little they have—whether she's happy about his plan or not.

Tasha, barely surviving an assassination attempt, is not sure who to trust. When Damon comes to check on her, she can only hope her instincts and her heart are right about him. This man meant everything to her for the years they'd worked together, but he'd always kept her at arm's reach. Now to learn that he and Terk are the only fully cognizant members of her old team, she wants to help but doesn't want to risk her life … again.

Still struggling with their new reality, both Tasha and Damon need to find out who did this to them. It's the only way to get their lives back—and to have a future together …

ICE POURED HERSELF a coffee and sat down at the compound's massive dining room table with the others. When her phone rang, she smiled at the number displayed. "Hey, Terk. How're you doing?" She put the call on Speakerphone.

"I'm okay," Terkel said, his voice distracted and tight.

"Terk?" Merk called from across the table. He got up and walked closer and sat across from Levi. "You don't sound too good, brother. What's up?"

"I'm fine," Terk said. "Or I will be. Right now, things are blown to shit."

"As in literally?" Merk asked.

"The entire group," Terk said, "they're all gone. I had a solid team of eight, and they're all gone."

"Dead?"

Several others stood to join them, gathered around Ice's phone. Levi stepped forward, his hand on Ice's shoulder. "Terk? Are they all dead?"

"No." Terk took a deep breath. "I'm not making sense. I'm sorry."

"Take it easy," Ice said, her voice calm and reassuring. "What do you mean, *they're all gone?*"

"All their abilities are gone," he said. "Something's happened to them. Somebody has deliberately removed whatever super senses they could utilize—or what we have been utilizing for the last ten years for the government." His tone was bitter. "When the US gov recently closed us down, they promised that our black ops department would never rise again, but I didn't expect them to attack us personally."

"What are you talking about?" Merk said in alarm, standing up now to stare at Ice's phone. "Are you in danger?"

"Maybe? I don't know," Terk said. "I need to find out exactly what the hell's going on."

"What can we do to help?" Ice asked.

Terk gave a broken laugh. "That's not why I'm calling. Well, it is, but it isn't."

Ice looked at Merk, who frowned, as he shook his head. Ice knew he and the others had heard Terk's stressed out tone and the completely confusing bits and pieces coming from his mouth. Ice said, "Terk, you're not making sense again. Take a breath and explain. Please. You're scaring me."

Terk took a long slow deep breath. "Tell Stone to open the gate," he said. "She's out there."

"Who's out there?" Levi asked, hopped up, looked outside, and shrugged.

"She's coming up the road now. You have to let her in."

"Who? Why?"

"*Because*," he said, "she's also harnessed with C-4."

"Jesus," Levi said, bolting to display the camera feeds to the big screen in the room. "Is it live?"

"It is, and she's been sent to you."

"Well, that's an interesting move," Ice said, her voice sharp, activating her comm to connect to Stone in the control room. "Who's after us?"

"I think it's rebels within the Iranian government. But it could be our own government. I don't know anymore," Terk snapped. "I also don't know how they got her so close to you. Or how they pinned your connection to me," he said. "I've been very careful."

"We can look after ourselves," Ice said immediately.

"But who is this woman to you?"

"She's pregnant," he said, "so that adds to the intensity here."

"Understood. So who is the father? Is he connected somehow?"

There was silence on the other end.

Merk said, "Terk, talk to us."

"She's carrying my baby," Terk replied, his voice heavy.

Merk, his expression grim, looked at Ice, her face mirroring his shock. He asked, "How do you know her, Terk?"

"Brother, you don't understand," Terk said. "I've never met this woman before in my life." And, with that, the phone went dead.

Find Book 1 here!
To find out more visit Dale Mayer's website.
smarturl.it/DMSTTDamon

Author's Note

Thank you for reading Bullard's Best: Bullard's Battle, Book 9! If you enjoyed the book, please take a moment and leave a short review.

Dear reader,

I love to hear from readers, and you can contact me at my website: www.dalemayer.com or at my Facebook author page. To be informed of new releases and special offers, sign up for my newsletter or follow me on BookBub. And if you are interested in joining Dale Mayer's Reader Group, here is the Facebook sign up page.
https://smarturl.it/DaleMayerFBGroup

Cheers,
Dale Mayer

Get THREE Free Books Now!

Have you met the SEALS of Honor?

SEALs of Honor Books 1, 2, and 3. Follow the stories of brave, badass warriors who serve their country with honor and love their women to the limits of life and death.

Read Mason, Hawk, and Dane right now for FREE.

Go here and tell me where to send them!
http://smarturl.it/EthanBofB

About the Author

Dale Mayer is a *USA Today* best-selling author, best known for her SEALs military romances, her Psychic Visions series, and her Lovely Lethal Garden cozy series. Her contemporary romances are raw and full of passion and emotion (Broken But ... Mending series). Her thrillers will keep you guessing (By Death series), and her romantic comedies will keep you giggling (*It's a Dog's Life*, a stand-alone novella; and the Broken Protocols series, starring Charming Marvin, the cat).

Dale honors the stories that come to her—and some of them are crazy and break all the rules and cross multiple genres!

To go with her fiction, she also writes nonfiction in many different fields, with books available on résumé writing, companion gardening, and the US mortgage system. She has recently published her Career Essentials series. All her books are available in print and ebook format.

Connect with Dale Mayer Online

Dale's Website – www.dalemayer.com
Twitter – @DaleMayer
Facebook – facebook.com/DaleMayer.author
BookBub – bookbub.com/authors/dale-mayer

Also by Dale Mayer

Published Adult Books:

Bullard's Battle
Ryland's Reach, Book 1
Cain's Cross, Book 2
Eton's Escape, Book 3
Garret's Gambit, Book 4
Kano's Keep, Book 5
Fallon's Flaw, Book 6
Quinn's Quest, Book 7
Bullard's Beauty, Book 8
Bullard's Best, Book 9

Terkel's Team
Damon's Deal, Book 1

Kate Morgan
Simon Says… Hide, Book 1
Simon Says… Jump, Book 2

Hathaway House
Aaron, Book 1
Brock, Book 2
Cole, Book 3

The K9 Files

Kurt, Book 12

Tucker, Book 13

Harley, Book 14

Kyron, Book 15

The K9 Files, Books 1–2

The K9 Files, Books 3–4

The K9 Files, Books 5–6

The K9 Files, Books 7–8

The K9 Files, Books 9–10

The K9 Files, Books 11–12

Lovely Lethal Gardens

Arsenic in the Azaleas, Book 1

Bones in the Begonias, Book 2

Corpse in the Carnations, Book 3

Daggers in the Dahlias, Book 4

Evidence in the Echinacea, Book 5

Footprints in the Ferns, Book 6

Gun in the Gardenias, Book 7

Handcuffs in the Heather, Book 8

Ice Pick in the Ivy, Book 9

Jewels in the Juniper, Book 10

Killer in the Kiwis, Book 11

Lifeless in the Lilies, Book 12

Murder in the Marigolds, Book 13

Nabbed in the Nasturtiums, Book 14

Offed in the Orchids, Book 15

Lovely Lethal Gardens, Books 1–2

Lovely Lethal Gardens, Books 3–4

Lovely Lethal Gardens, Books 5–6

Lovely Lethal Gardens, Books 7–8

Lovely Lethal Gardens, Books 9–10

Psychic Vision Series

Tuesday's Child

Hide 'n Go Seek

Maddy's Floor

Garden of Sorrow

Knock Knock...

Rare Find

Eyes to the Soul

Now You See Her

Shattered

Into the Abyss

Seeds of Malice

Eye of the Falcon

Itsy-Bitsy Spider

Unmasked

Deep Beneath

From the Ashes

Stroke of Death

Ice Maiden

Snap, Crackle...

What If...

Psychic Visions Books 1–3

Psychic Visions Books 4–6

Psychic Visions Books 7–9

By Death Series
Touched by Death
Haunted by Death
Chilled by Death
By Death Books 1–3

Broken Protocols – Romantic Comedy Series
Cat's Meow
Cat's Pajamas
Cat's Cradle
Cat's Claus
Broken Protocols 1-4

Broken and... Mending
Skin
Scars
Scales (of Justice)
Broken but... Mending 1-3

Glory
Genesis
Tori
Celeste
Glory Trilogy

Biker Blues
Morgan: Biker Blues, Volume 1
Cash: Biker Blues, Volume 2

SEALs of Honor

Mason: SEALs of Honor, Book 1

Hawk: SEALs of Honor, Book 2

Dane: SEALs of Honor, Book 3

Swede: SEALs of Honor, Book 4

Shadow: SEALs of Honor, Book 5

Cooper: SEALs of Honor, Book 6

Markus: SEALs of Honor, Book 7

Evan: SEALs of Honor, Book 8

Mason's Wish: SEALs of Honor, Book 9

Chase: SEALs of Honor, Book 10

Brett: SEALs of Honor, Book 11

Devlin: SEALs of Honor, Book 12

Easton: SEALs of Honor, Book 13

Ryder: SEALs of Honor, Book 14

Macklin: SEALs of Honor, Book 15

Corey: SEALs of Honor, Book 16

Warrick: SEALs of Honor, Book 17

Tanner: SEALs of Honor, Book 18

Jackson: SEALs of Honor, Book 19

Kanen: SEALs of Honor, Book 20

Nelson: SEALs of Honor, Book 21

Taylor: SEALs of Honor, Book 22

Colton: SEALs of Honor, Book 23

Troy: SEALs of Honor, Book 24

Axel: SEALs of Honor, Book 25

Baylor: SEALs of Honor, Book 26

Hudson: SEALs of Honor, Book 27

Lachlan: SEALs of Honor, Book 28

Heroes for Hire

SEALs of Steel

The Mavericks

Kerrick, Book 1

Griffin, Book 2

Jax, Book 3

Beau, Book 4

Asher, Book 5

Ryker, Book 6

Miles, Book 7

Nico, Book 8

Keane, Book 9

Lennox, Book 10

Gavin, Book 11

Shane, Book 12

Diesel, Book 13

Jerricho, Book 14

Killian, Book 15

Hatch, Book 16

The Mavericks, Books 1–2

The Mavericks, Books 3–4

The Mavericks, Books 5–6

The Mavericks, Books 7–8

The Mavericks, Books 9–10

The Mavericks, Books 11–12

Collections

Dare to Be You...

Dare to Love...

Dare to be Strong...

RomanceX3

Standalone Novellas
It's a Dog's Life

Riana's Revenge

Second Chances

Published Young Adult Books:

Family Blood Ties Series
Vampire in Denial

Vampire in Distress

Vampire in Design

Vampire in Deceit

Vampire in Defiance

Vampire in Conflict

Vampire in Chaos

Vampire in Crisis

Vampire in Control

Vampire in Charge

Family Blood Ties Set 1–3

Family Blood Ties Set 1–5

Family Blood Ties Set 4–6

Family Blood Ties Set 7–9

Sian's Solution, A Family Blood Ties Series Prequel
    Novelette

Design series
Dangerous Designs

Deadly Designs

Darkest Designs

Design Series Trilogy

Standalone

In Cassie's Corner

Gem Stone (a Gemma Stone Mystery)

Time Thieves

Published Non-Fiction Books:

Career Essentials

Career Essentials: The Résumé

Career Essentials: The Cover Letter

Career Essentials: The Interview

Career Essentials: 3 in 1

Made in the USA
Coppell, TX
21 December 2021

69866817R00085